MENSAH'S LONDON BLUES

and

OTHER STORIES

Austin Kaluba

First published in Great Britain in 2023 by:

Carnelian Heart Publishing Ltd
Suite A
82 James Carter Road
Mildenhall
Suffolk
IP28 7DE
UK

www.carnelianheartpublishing.co.uk

Paperback ISBN   978-1-914287-04-6
eBook ISBN   978-1-914287-05-3

A CIP catalogue record for this book is available from the British Library.

This collection of short stories is a work of fiction inspired by true events.

Editors:
Lazarus Panashe Nyagwambo
Samantha Rumbidzai Vazhure

Cover design & Layout:
Rebeca Covers

Typeset by Carnelian Heart Publishing Ltd
Layout and formatting by DanTs Media

To my late sister, Joyce Kaluba, for believing in me.

Table of Contents

Kippie Goes Home

"Mum, why did Kippie hang himself?" I asked my mother who was partially obscured by the mountain of clothes that she was washing. She straightened herself and scrubbed a stubborn collar stain, working her stubby fingers furiously.

The Zulu warrior song she'd been humming died in her throat.

"You will only understand when you grow up," she said.

"But why—"

"*Voetsek*!" She splashed me with suds, her chubby face angry now.

Fearing she would throw a bar of soap or some other missile at me as she was wont to do, I ran outside into the yard where embers were dying out on a brazier. The wind bit my face as I sauntered along Bertha Street, my hands thrust deep in my pockets. My right tennis shoe had a hole in it, and my toe, numb with cold, stuck out like a tortoise head. Up ahead, under a large oak tree, a small crowd had gathered, listening to a man in a heavy charcoal-grey coat.

"No longer shall this tree be the source of such misery!" said the man.

A few people nodded.

"There is a spirit that lives here. An evil spirit, in the bark, in the soil, in the branches that you see overhead!" he said, pointing up at the tree.

Unconsciously, I'd reached the spot where Kippie had hung himself the day before. The body had been taken away by the police early in the morning. I looked up at the tree and saw two pieces of thick rope, still wound round a lower branch. Knotted by Kippie's hands.

The police had cut the rope at head height.

"Cut it down!" said the man in the heavy coat.

Some of the crowd, bored now, moved off.

Kippie's tree had already gained a sinister reputation as the "Hanging Tree." Two other people who had been subject to forced removals from their homes in Sophiatown had swung their ropes over it in the past three months. Kippie always said, "No home, no respect. Every man needs a home." He'd lived with his grandmother.

I walked down the street and found Sandy throwing stones at Skippy, their mangy dog. Sandy had taken the dog three times to the white suburb to have it adopted by some white person there. But somehow the dog always found its way back to Sophiatown. The township was writhing with dogs that scrounged and snapped for food in rubbish dumps. They yanked at chicken bones and licked old packets and tins clean. I knew many residents who had rid themselves of their dogs in the white suburb. But Skippy went unclaimed.

"Sandy, stop throwing stones at the dog," I called out.

"Don't want it here."

Sandy's mother came out of the house and whistled, calling the dog by rubbing her right fingers against her thumb. Wagging its tail, the dog obeyed. She looked at it apologetically, as if sorry for trying to get rid of it.

I told Sandy about Kippie. He clapped his hands to his head in surprise, saying he'd had a bad dream where he saw people stabbing each other.

"But Kippie wasn't stabbed. He hanged himself," I said.

"There is no difference. Someone was stabbed in my dream, it could have been Kippie."

I did not want to argue. You could not win an argument with Sandy who talked so fast and always shouted above others.

I resumed walking down Bertha Street and Sandy accompanied me. At the corner, a man was playing a penny whistle for money. The melody was so plaintive that it brought tears to my eyes. If the collection of coins in the cup on the ground near his knee was an indication, others had also been moved by his music. As I tossed in a half a cent, the musician's eyes rose to meet mine and something in their expression reminded me of Kippie.

Kippie was kind of an outlaw but not a *tsotsi*. He was feared by everybody, including *tsotsis*, who left him alone whenever he walked the streets of Sophiatown with his colourful bell-bottomed trousers sweeping the ground and his biceps bulging against his vest. He'd always worn a menacing frown that distorted his ruggedly handsome features, but unlike other toughies on our street, Kippie had spoken good English. I had heard people say he'd been to college. It didn't surprise me. Despite his tough-guy exterior, I'd seen another side of Kippie, something pleasant that drew me to him.

It was the piano. I'd see him play Marabi a few times, his fingers pressing the keys with ease, his eyes straight ahead. He never gave public performances like other Marabi musicians who played at the Bantu Recreation Centre. It was said he composed most of the Marabi songs I heard bands singing in Sophiatown. Sandy had once told me it was Kippie who composed the popular Marabi hit "Hamba Khahle" which was about Goodson Khumalo, an ANC leader who had been shot dead by the police for organising a protest against forced removals.

Hamba Khale, we mnyama
Hamba Khale, son of Africa
Though departed, your soul lives on
Though gone, your struggle goes on
Hamba Khale, we mnyama
Amabunu ni inja
Hamba Khale, we mnyama.

One day Kippie showed me how to play one of the tunes. He said, "You try," and when I followed where his fingers went, he chuckled. "Ha!" he said. "You got it!"

I loved when he offered me the keys when I came by, moving out of the way so I could sit down, or even better, standing beside me while I played the bass notes he showed me so it was a duet. Kippie said I had natural talent. No one had ever said I was natural at anything before.

One day, I found Kippie sitting on the piano stool. I wanted to surprise him by tiptoeing behind his back, but he greeted me without turning. I asked how he had known it was me coming. He laughed and told me I had made a lot of noise.

He turned and motioned me to sit on the bed and I could tell that he didn't want me to play the piano or cards.

"How are you faring at school," he asked, still deep in thought.

"Fine," I answered, surprised at how different he looked on this day.

"Sipho, you must learn how to fight. Don't let life defeat you by accepting whatever the racist system throws at you." It was as if he was talking to himself.

I kept quiet because I felt the discussion was beyond me. He stood up and got a faded black and white picture from an old drawer. I saw him with several other students. Sipho was standing in the middle with a wide smile on his face. He looked at the picture for some time before putting it away. His face changed to that of a child about to cry. I bade my farewell and left.

Kippie lived with his grandmother in a two-room shack across from where I lived. They rented from a coloured landlord we only called Mr Jeffreys. Kippie would dust off his battered old cowboy hat and shout at me from his veranda in the mornings, "*Kunjani, mfana?*"

"Fine," I would answer, waiting for the predictable taunt.

"Going to school, heh. You want to be a lawyer or doctor?"

"I don't know."

"Then why are you going to school?"

Noticing my hesitation, he would double over laughing, his brown eyes glistening with tears of mirth. Unlike *tsotsis*, who bullied schoolchildren, Kippie showed some sort of affection for us though he also seemed to pity us for something I didn't understand until later.

I noticed a few months before Kippie died that many young men were wearing colourful blue, red and green bell bottoms. Some mimicked the way he talked, with a cigarette dangling from the corner of their mouth just like a cowboy. Everyone wanted to be a musician.

One Saturday, Kippie invited me to play cards with him on the veranda. I was unaware that my mother was watching me. She disapproved of anyone playing cards which she called the devil's game. "Sipho!" she hollered the moment I sat across from Kippie. "I say, Sipho, come here right now!"

Without looking up from the cards he was shuffling, Kippie spoke quietly, as if addressing himself. "Heh, boy, go back to your mother. She doesn't want you to end up a *tsotsi* or a good-for-nothing like me. You should finish school and get a decent job."

I felt a lump rise in my throat and ran back to my mother. From then on, whenever my mother was not around, I went over to Kippie's little room. I would often find him sitting on his bed with the cards in seven lines spread on a small table in front of him, playing Patience, or sometimes he'd be sitting at the piano, tinkling the keys. On those occasions, he seemed to be transported to another world, his face changing expression as he got carried away by the music.

"How is school, my young gentleman?" he would ask quietly without looking up.

I would say, "Good," because I knew it was the answer he wanted to hear. And the truth was I was doing well. I wasn't the best, but I was better than the middle.

"They teach you any songs?" he'd ask.

I'd tell him the choir songs we were learning, and he would tut. "Let me show you some real music," he'd say.

Sandy and I hung around the end of Bertha Street. The dog chased a crow and barked.

"That dog," said Sandy. "He's so stupid."

I didn't think the dog was stupid. He was just unloved.

After an hour of watching the world go by, we went our separate ways, and I came home. I was not home long when Kippie's grandmother put her head in the door. She was carrying a bible.

Kippie's grandmother was usually out selling at the market. She and Kippie had rarely spoken to one another but somehow got along well. She wore a scarlet shawl and kept the shack spotlessly clean. She looked twice her age though she walked with the grace and confidence of a person who had seen it all.

My mother indicated a bench she could sit on, but she chose a reed mat. Lowering herself, she opened the bible and removed a letter from it, wiping her brow with the end of her shawl. I saw the writing was in isiZulu.

"Esther, this is what Kippie left when he hung himself. Can you read it to me?"

"Au!" my mother exclaimed, clasping the sides of her head with both hands. She composed herself and took the letter into her trembling hand. Although I was seated a few feet away, I could see that the handwriting was beautiful and better than even that of my teacher, Mr Albert.

"Gogo, I also didn't go far in school. Maybe Sipho can read for us," Mother said, handing me the letter.

Surprisingly, my hands were steady. The two women fixed their gaze on me as I read Kippie's suicide note slowly:

> *Gogo,*
>
> *Don't blame me for what I have done. You know I love you and I know my action has broken your heart. Only if you knew, Gogo, how I feel after being expelled from college and being sucked back into Sophiatown to live off you when I am supposed to be looking after you. I thought education would be my only way out of squalor, but I was wrong. At college, my awareness of our plight as blacks was sharpened as I advanced in knowledge, and in the end, the very education that I thought would liberate me depressed me, leading to my organising a protest against our racist teachers.*
>
> *Once more, Gogo, forgive me.*
>
> *Kippie Khumalo.*

14

P.S. Can you give Sipho my piano? It is paid for.

I looked up, folding the page. The silence in the room was so deep that I could hear my heart beating. Kippie's grandmother took the letter from me, tucked it back into the bible and left without saying goodbye. Glancing at my mother, I saw tears in her eyes. Knowing how much she disliked me seeing her cry, I left our house and went to Sandy's.

He was sitting on the veranda, staring into space. There were members from the Anglican Church having a church service in their front room.

The women were singing the hymn, "How Sweet the Name of Jesus Sounds." I knew the chords on the piano. When I got Kippie's piano, I would play it for him.

Mensah's London Blues

I came to England as John Mensah, then I became Kofi Gyan, and later I came to be known as Kwame Ampiah. I was busted for my deception when my real name appeared in all the newspapers. My dark face popped out of the picture sheepishly, as if butter wouldn't melt in my mouth. The headlines mostly ran along the lines of "Illegal Immigrant Arrested for Drug Trafficking."

When I checked my inbox in the cooler, my notifications lit up red: 157 comments glared under an article about me from *The Daily Mail*, shared to my page by a girl who lived down my street back home. I had thrown a stone at her when she was six and I was seven.

Revenge.

The comments were a mixture of sympathy, anger and declarations that I had brought shame on my community. *Shame on this boy. Who raised him? Embarrassed for his family.*

The sympathetic comments came from people who knew me. From people who knew John Mensah. Not Kofi Gyan. Or Kwame Ampiah.

I'd had to change my name because I was using other people's documents to work. At first, I thought it was fun, but I quickly realised that something about a name sticks to you like a shadow or a soul. The first time I took on the name of Kofi, I felt like an amateur actor who couldn't get with his character.

At a warehouse where I worked, my boss called me one day by my assumed name. I was in the company of several other Africans. "Kofi! Kofi!" he shouted in my direction from a small office window. I didn't answer since I wasn't used to my new name, which was my cousin's, whose legal papers I was using at the time. The boss, some red-faced Irish bloke named O'Connor, came out from his small office and berated me for ignoring him. He thought I was being cheeky.

This name business is no small thing. I remember growing up in Lungni where elders told us not to shout somebody's name at night for fear witches would take it away and do harm to that person. I've often wondered if my name had been carried away. Was I cursed?

I scroll through all the comments then click on my inbox and my seventeen new messages. Friends that I sometimes chat to from home. A few strangers. Cousins. Some could never believe I had survived here for so long. I was ten years in England before I got caught.

The internet has made the world a much smaller place. In my inbox, I find a picture someone captioned with the words 'John Mensah OG.' Original gangster. The photo is one I posted myself a few years back when I went through a phase of posing with my arms folded, wearing sunglasses and a bowler hat. A mistake now, I realise. I've been telling people for so long how great this place is. I wonder how many saw through me.

I came here after I heard all the hip talk about the so-called good life everyone enjoyed in the United States, London and Paris. These fools did not tell us the other side of the story, about how they were breaking their backs to survive. Neither did they tell us how hard it is to pay rent and bills from one end of the day to the next. Water charges. Bus ticket. Lunch. Income tax. TV Licence. Gas bill. Council tax. Broadband. Electric. They didn't tell us that once they'd had enough of the crap, they went home where summer lasted all year long and life was simpler, full stop.

Those who went through more hell here were the worst culprits when it came to telling lies about Europe and the U.S. They talked as if whatever country was heaven on earth. I remember how they complained about everything back home in Accra, from the noisy minibuses and lack of proper garbage collection to the political corruption and the lousy state of the roads. Even the air, they said, stank. One guy, who claimed to have studied in the States (I later learned he worked as a janitor there), said he could not stand the sight of goats in town. They weren't necessarily wrong in their negative remarks; Accra did have all those problems, yes. But they spoke in such a showy manner that even the most unpatriotic Ghanaian couldn't help being annoyed.

Another guy like that who stands out in my memory was Kwame. He had huge biceps and preferred to call himself Don. He always dressed sharp, like some American rap star, cut-out in muscle T-shirts bearing pictures of long-dead musicians like Tupac Shakur and the Notorious B.I.G. His jeans swung dangerously low on his buttocks. He topped his outfits off with a cap worn sideways and gold rings flashing on his fingers. He greeted everybody with a "Hey, whassup?"

It was show-offs like this who made me decide to leave home for Europe. I started bothering my rich relatives to help me with cash to buy a ticket to go and study abroad. My cousin, Kofi, who had already been in England for many years wrote to me and advised that I stay in Ghana, explaining that things were not all they seemed abroad. I wrote back, asking if that was the case then why hadn't he come home?

The stories the show-off guys were telling got into my head, and I started looking at my town and country differently. This gradually grew into a slow burn hate. Each time I saw a goat nibbling in my garden, my thoughts cemented. Every time a cloud of smoke from a minibus rose up and choked me, I put another layer into my plan. I vowed that no matter what, I would get out.

I chose England because several friends from my town had sent pictures of themselves standing in places like Trafalgar Square or near Big Ben. They were all smiling foolishly in the snow with pigeons flying all over like moths around a streetlamp. Little did I know, these friends did jobs like caring for old people, or cleaning buildings, or they pulled duty at night as security guards. These are jobs even people with very little education like me detested back home. A friend told me about cheap bogus colleges in London that accepted students and gave them fake papers to take to the British Embassy to support their visa application. This I knew was my answer.

With not too much fuss, I found myself in London, attending classes in computer programming. After a few weeks, I went underground since my reason for attending the college had served its purpose. I joined other dudes and mommas who lived by their wits in an England most people don't know exists. Funny how England cuts you down to size. One of my Jamaican Rasta friends, Delroy, told me one day that "England is an open prison." At the time, I laughed. Now, I think about his words every night before I go to sleep.

I changed jobs like shirts, moving from warehouse operative to cleaner, carer, door bouncer, car washer. I even worked as a grave digger for a short while. I was always on the run from the authorities. Each time my employer started asking for stationery – that is what we call a visa, or the document giving leave to remain – I changed jobs or moved towns. Once, when things were really bad, a friend even suggested I register as a human guinea pig for medical testing. I discarded that idea when I read in the news how one eastern European bloke got ballooned up like an elephant after one of the experiments went wrong.

I rented single rooms in rundown places, many of which threatened to collapse. Others, I am sure, could have been condemned as not fit for even animal habitation. Most of these houses had been built during Queen Victoria's reign. The last time I rented a room was in East London. It was the cheapest place I could find. The landlord was a Nigerian who talked of living in almost every big city in the world and there were pictures to support his stories. He dressed like a pimp, with his fancy earrings, shiny suits, gold teeth and tattoos.

They called him The Duke or Obi. Like me, I suspect he had other aliases. I moved out from one of his dangerous pads when one day, coming home earlier than usual from my cleaning job, I found him in my bed with one of his many mistresses. When I raised hell, he shouted at me that it was his pad, and he had the right to use his rooms in any way he pleased. I shouted every curse word I could lay my tongue around. He got out of bed naked and came towards me. I backed away. Not because I was afraid of him. But because I'd never been chased by a man with an erection before. The following day, when I came home from work all my belongings sat outside in the rain and the locks had been changed. As I lifted my stuff and went to sit at a bus stop up the road, a familiar feeling crept in.

I was alone. And afraid. Not one person in the world knew how I was doing. And not one person cared. I could not go back home because I didn't have money for transport, and I had nothing to show for the time I had been in England. So I moved on.

I found another horrible room to rent, and I got up each day to carry boxes round a warehouse. I made one more futile attempt to legalise my stay. A lady-friend of mine who was old enough to be my auntie advised me to attend her church, The Heavenward Bound Ministries in Central London. The people there were really fanatics and promised that if one believed in God, anything could come true. *Anything* amounted to a veritable cocktail of requests for relief; from barrenness, impotence, bad luck, immigration problems and unemployment. Even stopping airplanes from crashing could be achieved by the proper prayer. I couldn't tell the difference between these guys and the witch doctors back home who claimed to cure all diseases!

Well, my *mami panyin* old woman invited me to one of their services and asked me to carry my passport, which had a long-expired visa. She said a man of God would bless it with special anointing oil to cause immigration officials to go blind and give me stationery. I couldn't help myself. Yes, I would go to church. Yes, I would give anything a try.

On Sunday, I put on a dark grey suit I had bought from an Oxfam charity shop and went to that church with my sugar mama. I was ready to be reborn. I was ready to be John Mensah once again. I remembered the words from a bumper sticker on a minibus back home: *Everything is possible under the sun*. In England, we rarely saw the bloody sun. Was I doomed?

I had the man of God bless my passport and he prayed for me too, shouting to God to intervene for a poor soul like me who had arrived in England by crossing oceans just to earn a living. He offered up a really emotional petition, breaking into tongues, blabbering, "Shakatuk, shakarakata, shakarakata, shakatuk."

I took the blessed passport home, wondering how I felt as the bus lurched from stop to stop. What did my stomach tell me? Would this work? Could I be saved?

That evening I wrote a letter and dropped it over to my better-educated cousin, Kofi, to proofread. "All good," he said. The next day, I sent the anointed passport with the letter pleading with the Home Office to be given an indefinite stay. I explained that I had been in the country for so long already, that I had become a natural citizen, and I'd paid my dues.

To my surprise, the Home Office replied rather fast. Two days later, I came home from work to find a white envelope on the hall window waiting for me. I tore it open, standing in the crusty hall that smelled of mould. Somebody had put a little jar of oil with skinny sticks in it on the window to try and hide the smell so now the mould was tainted with sandalwood.

The letter said that the grounds I had given for being awarded permanent stay were very weak. Or as they put it: *We are sorry to inform you that your request has been denied due to insufficient reasons.* They also wanted to know if the address I used was correct since they had lost track of my whereabouts. I got my stuff and left that evening. Back to the bus stop again.

The following week, I decided to go back to my immigration lawyer, to whom I had already paid a considerable sum, to see if he could fix it so I could live freely without constantly looking over my shoulder. He promised me heaven and wrote a very expensive letter for me. Then he wrote a follow up in exchange for more of my hard-earned money. I drew another blank from the Home Office.

My friends suggested I marry an Eastern European woman. Having exhausted all other avenues, I decided that out of everything, this might not be so bad. I went through an agency run secretly by a Nigerian in conjunction with an eccentric vicar. Some of my friends said the two men, whom I later learned were confirmed criminals, had helped many people by marrying them in the Church of England whose head was the Queen herself.

The woman I was to marry was a Polish girl with an unpronounceable name full of consonants and letters I never even knew could go together. On D-day, I went to the registry office with my bride who was unusually shy and only spoke monosyllabically like some child just learning how to speak. She wore a suit that hung large on her skinny frame. I wondered if, in the real world, I could really have her as my wife. Could I go to bed with her? Have her wash my clothes? Could I teach her English and together we could communicate in childish, fidgety laughter?

But she did not smile. Her lips stayed in a solid line. To make up for her demeanour I did my best to look pleasant, and when the registrar asked did I take her as my wife, I nodded and smiled as brightly as I could. My 'best man' was a bloke from Lithuania who had been hastily tutored for his role on the big day. He was wearing trainers and a tracksuit top and bottoms that clashed, making the entire affair resemble a circus act. He held withered flowers in his hands.

The registrar went through his thing about marriage being a union only ending in death. When he was through, we were declared husband and wife. I kissed my bride rather noisily and clumsily and felt her recoil from me. I breathed a sigh of relief now that my sorrows were over. Boy was I mistaken.

Word came that the Home Office would be investigating the circumstances under which I had married my Polish wife. Since I was not living with her, the one whose name I couldn't even pronounce properly, I decided to run. At the same time, to my chagrin, I read a story in the papers about the jailing of the registrar and his Nigerian accomplice.

I sat in my lonely room contemplating what to do. I thought of handing myself to the Home Office for repatriation. Then another thought of what I would do in Ghana if I was repatriated entered my mind. I knew everyone would laugh at me for going back home empty-handed.

I remembered a fable I had read back home about an owl that wanted to be downstairs and upstairs at the same time.

I decided I wouldn't make yet another attempt to legalise my stay. Everyone had failed me. Not even God, it seemed, could change the outcome of my status. I was tired of doing menial work that paid a pittance. What was the use of doing shit jobs if I couldn't get legal status? I started to think that if I was going to be an illegal immigrant then why not look to illegal money too? I knew I would be better off. I had nothing to lose since I was already taking a risk living here without the proper papers.

I had enough headaches to end up in a mental home. Pierre, my friend from Mauritius, went cuckoo just like that. He started hearing voices. One of them was telling him to kill his dog, while another told him to drink his piss, and a third wanted him to strip. I didn't want to go mad. But if I didn't change something, I felt that I might.

I had a few connections who I knew dealt in marijuana. You started small, doing a few transactions to build up trust, and once they knew you were legit, you got more to sell.

The first time I made a haul, I quit my cleaning job. My boss phoned me in the middle of the night and told me about an extra shift. I said I was no longer interested in cleaning toilets. He started shouting, and I told him to go fuck himself. I lay back on my pillow and smiled.

From marijuana, I went to coke. From coke I went to skag. I had methadone, benzos and a connection who could get enough prescription oxy to knock out an elephant.

The drug business was a way out. The money was good. With the drugs came the women. I bought them jewellery, lingerie and paid for the best hotels we could find on the internet. We drank and did coke so we could drink some more. I felt like I was a porn star. This was the life I'd come to England for.

And then, I got nabbed. Red handed. Found myself in Her Majesty's Prison. Sometimes I wondered if my old cleaning boss had something to do with it. Had he reported me? Who had squealed? These English courts don't waste time with adjournments like they do back home. During the sentencing, it was made clear that my "type" was not wanted in England. Although the man of the law did not name the place where he believed my kind could be tolerated, I knew he meant Africa.

As I was led away, back down the stairs to the prison cells, I heard myself shouting, "Bastards! You know nothing! This fucking place, man! You know nothing about me!" My tirade was directed against the judge. Against the prosecutor.

Against the smug smirk on their faces when they told me through their body language and legalese to go back to where I came from.

My cousin, Kofi, was in court when that bespectacled, pink-faced judge handed down my sentence. He was sympathetic, I knew, but I was beyond being sympathised with. Kofi, the perpetual student in England, always lectured me about how tough this place was. He once told me: "We're all slaves. Just our brothers were brought here in chains. We booked an air ticket." Typical Kofi, always studying and saying wise things. He is different from my other cousin, Caroline who thinks she is British and dresses and speaks like an Englishwoman. She pronounces the names of English cities and towns as if they are heavenly places. For example, she would swallow the t when pronouncing places like Luton and Gatwick. She is full of stupidity, acting as if back home in Ghana she wasn't just a waitress.

Recently, some white guy who writes books came here to teach inmates who wanted to learn the craft. I joined the class out of boredom. The man insisted we should write about what we knew, so after attending a few of those lessons, I wrote this piece. I showed it to the man, and he said I had broken one important rule, namely, of writing by telling and not by showing. He said, however, that he liked the story because it was original and from the heart. I am not educated like Kofi, but that hasn't stopped me from telling my story. Surprisingly, I feel more at home in prison, apart from the lingering thought that I might be deported after doing my time.

Maybe it was God's will that I should have been busted because I could have ended up dead. I don't care what those wankers will say when I arrive home with nothing but my balls. I might tell some bastards who would bother to hear me that they should forget about all the crap we hear and the pictures of rich people enjoying themselves on beaches we see back home. I know a number of fools would ask me why I stayed so long if things weren't working. As I am writing this in the cooler room, I know people are queuing at the British Embassy for papers to come over to this open prison called England.

Auntie Agatha's Quest

Aunt Agatha was in the living room, examining an emerald-green evening gown she had just bought from Debenhams. She stretched the gown lengthwise against her slim body while she extended her left foot forward. The gown seemed to be the right size.

"Heh, Lameck. Look at what I have here," she said. She looked tired. Last night, Miss Chanda, her friend, had stayed late for dinner.

"Good gown, Auntie," I replied.

"It is an evening gown. Friends have invited me to a party in London next week."

Clothes bulged from several bags bearing different shop names: Next, BHS and Marks & Spencer. She had also bought two books from Waterstones: one was Danielle Steele's *Impossible*, and the other was a book titled *Watching The English* by Kate Fox. She brought her purchases to the bedroom and closed the door.

Aunt Agatha had just failed her Form Three examinations when she married my uncle Tom back in Zambia. In England, she had sat for the University of London GCE O-level examinations but failed each time. My uncle spent a good deal of time trying to help her with her studies, but all was in vain.

Auntie, as I called her, was a petite, light skinned, pretty woman with a gap between her two front teeth and prominently high cheekbones. I wouldn't say I liked or disliked her. I found her interesting, despite how she would often reduce me to the role of assistant in her domestic chores.

Our family did not approve of Uncle Tom's choice. They expected him to marry an educated woman, preferably a doctor. However, Uncle had always been a rebel in his silent way.

Shortly after marrying, the couple had a baby boy called Kelvin. Tongues wagged. Clearly, conception had taken place prior to the nuptials.

I must have been fourteen or fifteen years old, completing the seventh grade, when I first visited them at Emmasdale in Lusaka. They had a modern three bed-roomed house. Although Agatha was a taskmaster, I found her company preferable to that of my cruel stepmother who treated me like a slave. During my first visit, I helped Auntie with babysitting while she knitted a shawl for the infant.

Uncle Tom was a doctor who taught medicine at the hospital attached to the University of Zambia. Being a teacher at the hospital meant coming home late every night, tired. He would eat his meal and retire to his bedroom or sometimes go to the living room where he read the *Times of Zambia* and *Newsweek*. He sometimes listened to jazz records by the likes of Duke Ellington, Billie Holliday, John Coltrane, and Miles Davis.

It was Aunt Agatha who ruled the roost. Family members said he was under what they called a 'petticoat government'. Needless to say, she was unpopular among our family members, especially the womenfolk, who nicknamed her The Wasp. I don't know if it was my stepmother who gave her the moniker, but it suited her. She had a slender waist and a big behind just like a wasp. And yes, she stung from time to time.

My stepmother and Aunt Agatha did not get on. My stepmother thought Agatha stupid and lecherous, pawning off our Uncle. Aunt Agatha sensed the family's resentment but kept it all boiled up for my stepmother. Whenever they met it would end with one of them taking major offence. It was just a matter of who.

That first summer when I was spending my school holiday with my Aunt and Uncle, my stepmother, who was a retired headmistress, came to visit to see the baby. I had just passed my examinations to attend secondary school; I had graduated from wearing shorts to trousers. My stepmother knew that I did a lot of chores for Aunt Agatha and she complained and asked what exactly the 'Missus' did if I did all the work. I wanted to tell her that she worked me harder than Aunt Agatha and her wrath was a bit hypocritical.

"You did not come here to be a slave!" she said one morning when she found me in the living room, scrubbing the floor. The baby was in a child's pen, lying on his back, kicking his legs. The kitchen door was partially open and I could see Aunt Agatha moving towards the sink. She wore a skimpy scarlet red silk dress that showed off her wasp waist and large, milk-filled breasts. My stepmother wore a *chitenge*-wrapper, matching her head scarf. "Times have changed, my son. Education is now everything. You need to be educated like Tom and marry an educated woman befitting your education."

I kept quiet since I knew she was not addressing me. Aunt Agatha coughed noisily and called, "Lameck! Lameck! I say, Lameck. Are you deaf?"

"Coming, Auntie," I answered, tossing the scrubbing brush into the bucket of water. In the kitchen, my aunt gave me some crisp paper notes.

"Go and buy me some beers from the tavern," she said, raising her voice. She gave me a bag with eight empty Mosi bottles to return. I ran to the tavern and came back with the new beers which I put in the fridge. I saw a stock of beers in there and wondered why she had asked me to buy more. My stepmother sat in the living room watching the baby, her arms folded and a murderous expression on her face. I knew she wanted to say something to both of us.

My aunt started drinking. She drank straight from the bottle. I knew my stepmother would never do such a thing; in our house, you couldn't even put a glass down without a coaster. She also increased the volume on the ITT Supersonic radio in the kitchen which was playing a repeat programme by Timmy Mvula. She stood up and wriggled around to the music. Then she poured me Coca-Cola in a glass, saying, "Here drink this."

I was torn between the two women, though I found myself siding with my stepmother more out of respect for her age. I hated myself for not mustering enough courage to silence my aunt whom I thought was being disrespectful. At the same time, I felt my stepmother lacked tact in the way she addressed her younger in-law. The thrill of the tension filled up my stomach along with the Coca-Cola. My stepmother mistreated me at home. Here, Aunt Agatha mistreated my stepmother.

At three beers, my stepmother had come into the kitchen and counted the bottles, her eyes flickering; one, two, three. She sighed and banged about the place, making a cup of tea. She asked if I had nothing better to do than sitting on my back-side drinking Coca-Cola. But again, I knew the comment was not meant for me.

At five beers, Auntie it seemed, could not contain the effect of the alcohol because her speech became slurred, and she staggered slightly. My stepmother came into the kitchen, still brooding and said the baby needed feeding. She pushed me out of the way and got a dustpan from the corner of the room. My auntie was about to get her sixth beer from the fridge when my stepmother grabbed her hand. The younger woman pushed away, and before long they stood facing each other like two angry tigresses.

"You can't keep a home if you keep yourself busy drinking instead of housekeeping," my stepmother said.

"What is it to you if I drink and how much I drink?" retorted my aunt.

"You are not fit to be a mother!"

"You are also not fit to be an in-law if you come here to spy on your daughter-in-law."

"Let your stupid husband come. I am sure you have given him a love potion to keep an untutored woman like you!"

"Who is untutored?" my aunt shouted, glaring at her adversary.

"You, of course! You are untutored!" my stepmother shouted back.

"If I am untutored, then you are also untutored," my aunt said.

"Me?" my stepmother asked, pointing at herself.

"Who else would I be talking to?"

"How dare you insult me?" My stepmother glared at my auntie.

I rushed between them to break them apart. My aunt went to the living room to pick up the baby, shouting obscenities, while my stepmother sat in the kitchen, crying.

She remained there until Uncle Tom came. She narrated to him what had happened and insisted on being driven back to the station for her to go back home. After pleading with her to change her mind, he finally obliged, and my stepmother left without saying goodbye to us.

After her departure, I could see that my uncle was unusually quiet and retired to bed earlier than usual. I also failed to hide my indignation at what had happened to my stepmother and did not take out the bins like Auntie asked. Auntie became more attentive to our needs. She kissed Uncle Tom over and over on the cheek.

After Uncle had read the English dailies, my aunt would go through them slowly and pick any topical story which she would later discuss with neighbours or visitors.

I remember one time on a Saturday when two of my uncle's friends, Dr Moonga and Mr Tembo, came to visit, my uncle angrily flung the copy of *The Times* on the table. It had a story about a bombing in Mkushi.

"Smith is mad if he thinks the minority whites can continue ruling Rhodesia," Uncle said, taking a swig from his glass.

"He once said there will never be a black government in a thousand years. Damn racist pig," Dr Moonga cut in, a chuckle rocking his bulky frame.

Unnoticed by the trio, my aunt had slipped into the living room with a glass of Coke and brandy that she had been drinking in the kitchen while cooking. She was getting drunk; I could tell by the expression on her face. She looked wistful and her eyes were glassy. She seemed eager to join in the discussion. Sensing that his wife was somehow out of place, my uncle switched to ciBemba, a local dialect. My aunt's face brightened and I could tell she was looking for an opportune time to contribute to the discussion.

Dr Moonga was talking of the need for other African countries joining hands to chase all whites from Rhodesia. His ciBemba was very poor, and he put in several English words from time to time.

"Can someone tell me what these missiles want in our country?" my aunt cut in. I knew she meant rebels, but the two words always appeared together in the newspapers. I could see my uncle was embarrassed. Dr Moonga pretended not to have heard the question, while Mr Tembo showed a flicker of amusement but quickly masked it when he saw nobody else was laughing. Fortunately, my aunt had already moved onto the skyrocketing prices of essentials.

On paydays, my aunt did the shopping in duty-free shops which dealt in dollars when the majority of Zambians were buying in Kwacha. Instead of cheap drinks like Kwench and TipTop, we enjoyed canned Coca-Cola and Fanta. My aunt kept the empty cans on display in the window and reserved a few drinks which she only served when her friends visited. I could tell she enjoyed their surprise when she produced such rare commodities.

When Zambian doctors started fleeing for greener pastures after the economy got worse, my aunt pestered my uncle to try his luck in England. They left in 1992, shortly after Kaunda was removed from power. They settled in Manchester.

When I finished school and after a whole summer of pestering my uncle to send for me, a plane ticket was booked and I had an escape from my stepmother. I was to help my aunt with the children, as they had a new baby, their third called Mapalo.

If I settled and liked England, they would look at enrolling me in university. I wanted to do everything to stay.

In Manchester, my uncle still spoke like any down-to-earth Zambian back home, while Aunt Agatha now spoke in a high nasal accent she thought was good English. When giving me my flight details over the phone, I had to keep saying "I beg your pardon" because I could not understand her.

When I arrived in England in February, I was wearing a heavy coat because my aunt had warned me that it would be very cold. She was not wrong. My teeth chattered and the tips of fingers turned hot and numb. A taxi they had pre-booked took me to my aunt and uncle's house.

My uncle opened the door for me and shook hands, greeting me in *ciBemba*. My aunt, who had rounded in a matronly way, nodded a greeting in my direction. Her smile did not reach her eyes.

To my surprise, my uncle, whom I had known never to object to whatever my aunt did, reprimanded her in *ciBemba*. "*Efyo uposha abantu ifyo?*" – Is that the way you greet people? She put down the glass she was holding and came over to shake my hand.

The street where my aunt and uncle lived looked posh with trees lined up outside and expensive looking cars parked all along the street. Kelvin, whom I had babysat in Zambia, was now a lanky six year old and he sat playing a video game in the corner. Misodzi, who had only been a baby when they left Zambia, sat beside him, watching. Both of them ignored me. Mapalo, was in an elaborate Moses basket which had a drape that hung down, almost like a mosquito net. I went over to look inside.

My uncle's phone rang and he left the room.

"Open that window, it is warm in here," commanded my aunt.

I opened up the window reluctantly even though it was the peak of winter and freezing outside.

A draught rushed in, making me feel cold to the bone. I looked at my aunt who seemed to be enjoying my discomfort. It was as though she were pretending to be an Englishwoman, immune to such cold.

Auntie went to make tea and when she came back, I loaded two large teaspoons of sugar into my cup. I noticed that Auntie took none.

"Don't you take sugar?" I asked.

"Never touch it," she said.

In Zambia, Auntie had always loaded her tea with sugar. It seemed there had been much change, great and small.

We sipped our teas until Uncle came back in. He rushed to the window and closed it. "Are you not freezing?" My aunt kept quiet while I pretended not to hear the question.

Aunt Agatha's phone, which was on a charger, rang. It was Miss Chanda, as I saw her name on the screen. Miss Chanda had come to England when Zambia Airways closed, leaving a good number of staff unemployed. After the airline closed, I began to hear about a new disease called 'depression'.

"Hello, Angela," my aunt answered.

"Hi, Agatha," I faintly heard Miss Chanda's voice from the other end.

"My hubby has just come in complaining of the cold! How is London?" my aunt asked.

"That is the problem with Zambians," I heard the tinny voice say. "*Ubututu*."

Aunt Agatha put her hand over the phone to ask my Uncle what he wanted to eat for dinner.

"*Nshima* with chicken," my uncle said.

Aunt Agatha went back to her conversation with Miss Chanda, leaving the room to go to the kitchen. "I went to a party last night…"

I stayed in the sitting room watching the boys killing blood soaked zombies.

Uncle Tom wanted all the news from home.

That weekend, Miss Chanda visited. She arrived dressed gaudily in an orange blouse and a black skirt. Wearing heavy makeup, she looked older than her years. Ugly blotches circled her eyes, a result of many years of using lightening creams.

The two hugged in a theatrical way, kissing one another on the cheeks. My aunt took off Miss Chanda's coat and hung it on the rail before ushering her visitor into the living room. She had made me spruce it up, dusting the skirting boards and vacuuming the rug twice.

Miss Chanda seemed anxious, like someone who had something important to announce. As the two sat down, I fixed them some spirits: Coke and brandy for my Auntie and Amarula for Miss Chanda. I sat with them in the living room, watching a repeat episode of *Strictly Come Dancing*. I lowered the volume of the TV with the remote.

I got the intense feeling that both women wanted me to go. It was as if they had something to discuss and they did not want me, a young man, to listen.

Still, I stayed.

"I have been promoted to supervise other nurses," said Miss Chanda. "The job is very involving, but I am enjoying it."

"That's great," my aunt replied half-heartedly.

She got up and paced about the room.

Miss Chanda adjusted herself in the seat, crossing her legs as she sipped her Amarula. "Are you in touch with home, Agatha?"

"No. Once in a while I talk to some people. Too many beggars asking for money."

"Ha. I have become part of Western Union outlets."

"Yeah. I have also cut many out. I only talk to my mother," Aunt Agatha said.

"Those people don't know how we sweat for the money, us who work," said Miss Chanda.

"If I worked, I would retire early. I wouldn't want to end up demented," my aunt said.

"The pension is good in old age, though."

Miss Chanda looked on, far away in thought. Then she spoke, "I bought an aquarium. I have six goldfish. Damn expensive to feed."

My aunt sighed and stared at me.

Eventually, when the room grew silent, I got up to leave.

Being in my room was better than being stuck between two older women who wanted me out of the way.

Miss Chanda stayed until late in the evening, and we had supper. Aunt called it "dinner". When she left, she gave my aunt a lingering hug on the doorstep.

The next morning, my auntie went out shopping, returning with the bulging bags of clothes and her new books. After a while, I heard a commotion in her room. I listened outside the door and realised that my auntie was vomiting.

"Auntie?" I called. "Are you okay?"

There was no response. Carefully I opened the door.

The door to her ensuite bathroom was open and I could hear more vomiting.

"Auntie," I said.

Reluctantly, I walked into the ensuite.

Noticing my presence, she tried to say something, but a gush of vomit prevented her. She threw up a white, slimy substance. Her face looked pale.

"Leave me," she spluttered.

I left the ensuite and saw the emerald-green gown spread on the bed. She had vomited on it too, the white splashed all over the dark green.

My uncle had long gone for work. I didn't know what to do. The children were at school, but the baby was grizzling in his Moses basket.

She had removed herself from the bathroom now and was lying, half on top of the green dress. She let out a long moan.

"Auntie?" I said. "Auntie?"

I went back out to the living room, took up my phone and called my Uncle. Trying to explain my aunt's symptoms I told him that she was vomiting and I didn't know what to do.

"It must be a bug. Phone an ambulance," he said. I called the ambulance and knelt beside Auntie who had stopped convulsing and was lying motionless on the bed. Her eyes were blank. I heard a distant siren which grew louder by the moment.

The ambulance arrived, and two men in green uniforms came in. The taller man asked me what had happened and examined Auntie. They shone a tiny torchlight into her eyes and quickly strapped her to the stretcher and lifted her outside. I wanted to accompany them, but they told me I could not take the baby.

My aunt was admitted to the hospital. My uncle went straight to the hospital and came home hours later. He did not tell me much, only that Aunt Agatha would be alright. He took the baby and held it under his chin, staring into the distance.

During visiting hours the next day, we surrounded her bed, trying to talk to her, but to no avail. She rolled from side to side screaming in *ciBemba*, "*Nafwa mayo mutuule mwe bantu!*" – I am dying, Mother. Please help.

My uncle held her hand, saying, "Agatha, calm down. You will soon be okay," but it was to no avail.

My aunt continued rolling and crying. "*Ntwaleni kumwesu eko nkaye fwila. Teti mfwile mwanabene. We chalo uli mukali.*" – Take me home to die. I don't want to die in a foreign land. Oh, what a cruel world.

Miss Gondwe and Miss Daka bowed their heads solemnly.

An African nurse with tribal marks came and tried to give Aunt some tablets, but she could not open her mouth.

"Let's pray," Mrs Daka said. We all closed our eyes as Miss Daka prayed for my aunt's speedy recovery. She asked God to cause all the principalities of darkness to depart. She continued praying until I was not only conscious of her prayers but of my breathing. Finally, she said "Amen," to which we echoed, "Amen" in return.

Outside the hospital, Miss Daka consoled my uncle, explaining that my aunt would be alright because she was only having "women problems".

Three days after my aunt was discharged from hospital, I heard shouting coming from my aunt and uncle's bedroom. My aunt rushed out, pursued by my uncle who was dressed in his gown.

"Why didn't you tell me the truth, you bitch!" My uncle raised his fist, poised to strike.

My aunt covered her face with her hands.

"I am busy at work, and you are busy sleeping with white men!"

"Forgive me, Tom," my aunt sobbed, cowering in the corner of the living room.

The two older boys were on the sofa. They stopped playing their game and their eyes turned into saucers.

"You're a disgrace!"

"Forgive me, Tom," my aunt sobbed.

"I wish you had died together with the baby you aborted. You are such a disgrace!"

I went to my room and heard Uncle Tom slamming the bedroom door. I could hear my aunt's sobbing. After the row, the two stopped talking to each other. My uncle prepared his own meals and ate alone. My aunt still ate with me, but there was no conversation between us.

For some reason, I started phoning my stepmother more regularly. I started warming up to her.

Two weeks later, my aunt applied for the GCSEs again.

This time, she says she will pass.

Maria's Vision

Maria's heart beat hard as she stirred the thickening *sadza* with a practised, gentle motion. She repeatedly glanced at the wall-clock hanging in the kitchen, pouring mealie-meal into the silver pot, letting it run out of her hand like sand in an hourglass.

The clock seemed to be moving faster than usual as both its long and short hands approached twelve, the time her husband returned home from his shift. She had already prepared the chicken stew, just the way Tapiwa liked it – thick and spicy. As she stirred the *sadza*, she read a story about Zimbabwe from an open page of *The Guardian*.

The story was accompanied by a picture of an ox-drawn ambulance with wobbly wheels and a pitiful-looking ox, like the one Pharaoh had dreamed about in the Bible. The ox's mournful eyes seemed to plead to be relieved of the giant, crude yoke laid on its scrawny shoulders. This was the transport that was being used in many parts of rural Zimbabwe to convey the sick to hospital. The patient pictured on the stretcher looked as hopeless as the ox, with his concertina-like ribs showing through a *chitenge* cloth, his eyes partially closed.

As Maria took in the picture, the sounds and smells of her native country flooded her senses. She heard the cluck, cluck of the wheel turning on the ox-drawn ambulance. She saw the red brown soil over which the cart rolled and the scrubby trees that dotted the invalid's journey to hospital. Now that was all left behind. Now, there were concrete and stone buildings and ambulances covered in neon checkerboard.

Maria shook her head and sighed and considered herself lucky to have escaped the grinding poverty in Zimbabwe. England was a country she had once only read about in books. Now she was here, living a relatively peaceful life where she didn't have to worry about daily increases of food prices or shortages of fuel and electricity.

In the distance, a siren sounded, then grew louder on approach. A neon ambulance or a fire engine? A police car perhaps? Relatively peaceful. Was it?

Maria and her husband lived in a two-bedroom house in Hatfield, along St Alban Road, with baby Chichi. The house was quite plush although it was marred somewhat by a fly-tip on the derelict waste ground behind their house that was regularly added to.

Broken baby push-chairs, sofas, a half-burnt Yamaha motor bike, soiled and mouldy boots, piles of wood left over from construction sites, all found their way to the other side of Maria's back wall.

Every morning when she opened the curtains, it was the first thing that greeted her.

As she held her cup of coffee in the kitchen while Chichi played bricks on the floor, she looked out at the increasing pile of debris.

It didn't seem to bother her husband. It was if he didn't even see it; the mess, the junk. The unsightliness of it all.

Now Chichi, who had been sleeping peacefully on the sofa for the past twenty minutes, moaned and moved. She turned in her sleep, forcing the book of fairy tales that had been resting on her chest to fall to the floor.

Maria pulled the pot of *sadza* off the stove and walked over to her daughter. She lifted her gently and went to put her on the bed upstairs. She glanced at the bedside clock; it

43

was nearly half past twelve. She rushed downstairs to finish preparing the meal. A car pulled up outside. Then the front door opened quietly as Tapiwa made his way in. Always, he came in quietly, as if hoping to catch her in some sort of mischievous act. Each time the door opened, she felt her hairs stand on end.

Moments later, he stood at the kitchen door, watching her without a word of greeting. His long, dark face contrasted with the white background of the room. He took off his heavy coat and pulled a dining chair to the table.

"How was work?" Maria addressed him in English.

"Okay," he replied in Shona, wearing a frown that his wife was now used to.

She wanted to go upstairs to check on Chichi but knew that he would take offence if she left. As she put the tray of food and a small dish of water in front of her husband, she smelled the sweat from his armpits.

"Where is Chichi?" he asked, without looking up from his meal.

"Sleeping."

"Has she eaten?"

"Yes."

"And you?" he enquired, pointing at her with a fistful of *sadza*.

"I have eaten, too," she answered as she pulled out a chair and sat opposite her husband.

He grunted and concentrated on his food, stuffing lumps of *sadza* into his mouth and swallowing with a great deal of noise. Halfway through his meal, he raised his head, taking notice of Maria as though he had just remembered that she was at the table with him. Then, half-sarcastically, he commented, "You

have become a proper English woman in a black skin, huh?"
Pausing briefly to swallow the bits of remaining food in his
mouth, he continued, "You no longer want to eat with your
husband. You want to eat alone with your child."

"What's wrong with me eating alone?" Maria asked,
raising her voice. "And remember, it is *our* child, not *my*
child."

"You could never have spoken to me in such a manner
back home. The British culture has taught you to answer
your husband so cheekily!" His voice rose over hers.

"What is cheeky about reminding you that Chichi is our
child?" she asked more softly, trying to sound contrite.

"What is wrong with answering back when your
husband is talking?" He repeated the question in a mocking
tone.

Maria kept quiet.

Tapiwa finished his meal and switched on the TV. He
changed channel after channel till he settled on a repeat
boxing match between Daryl Harrison and Danny
Williams. He moved his head at the landing of each punch
from the two boxers. Maria hated finding herself with such
a difficult man. She had thought long and hard about how
she could end her miserable marriage, especially now that
she was in Britain where divorce was easier than back home.
But something always held her back, not least of all the fear
of shaming her family and acting contrary to her Christian
faith.

And then there was Chichi. She did not want Chichi
growing up in a separated family. Each time she looked at
her, she felt a pang of guilt for not choosing a better man.
Now, they were stuck. Now, she could only get on with
things as best she could.

Maria had met Tapiwa while she was teaching in Harare. He was working as an accountant for Zimbabwe Airlines. She had gradually grown to like him, perhaps because he reminded her of her late father. Like him, Tapiwa was tall, dark, and muscular. But that's where the similarities ended. Her father had had an easy-going personality and had been slow to anger. Tapiwa was reserved and seemed to go through life suspecting that everybody was his enemy or somehow disapproved of him. Early in their marriage, when they were back home in Zimbabwe, she realised how jealous he was when he beat her for talking to Tambudzai, a former classmate. The beating had left her with a black eye, two loose teeth, and a very damaged ego.

What annoyed her even more was the attitude of law enforcement when she went to the local police station to report the assault. One policeman had outright told her that they could not intervene in a domestic affair, even though her face was swollen. When leaving the station, she overheard a younger officer commenting about her beauty. "The man should not mess up that woman's face. She is so beautiful. If I was her husband, I would be staying home all day."

The women neighbours were of little help. She had overheard one of them telling her friend that modern wives lacked the stamina of their mothers who could take blows boldly. To prove their point, the women had sung a popular marriage counselling song in Shona. Maria remembered the lines:

> *Listen you untutored whore:*
> *The husband is your lord and protector;*
> *someday, he can give you loving slaps;*
> *don't cry out and wake the neighbourhood.*

It is your silence we respect, not your howling;
loving slaps strengthen the marriage;
loving slaps, that is the name of the game.

As Tapiwa watched the boxing match, Maria found herself thinking back to that first beating. She smiled in mockery at the words of the songs. Imagine, that was what they were taught? Imagine singing that to Chichi? As soon as she caught herself smiling, she realised that her husband was watching her.

"Why are you smiling to yourself?" he demanded.

"I remembered something," she said, looking away.

"What is that something?" he asked, his voice tight.

Maria shook her head. "Nothing."

Nothing.

She waited, waiting for him to turn back to the TV and when he did, she felt relieved and withdrew into her own world.

Her skin was still on end.

Always, it was on end around him.

Tapiwa was still watching TV when Maria went upstairs to check on Chichi. He did not seem to notice her slip away and so, she lay on the bed and rested. When Chichi awoke from her nap, she tickled her tummy and blew raspberries on her sweet skin.

Chichi giggled and laughed, pushed her mother away and then offered her belly for more. Maria was working the afternoon shift. She hated leaving the baby with Tapiwa. She knew he would not be kind in the way that she was kind. Chichi would cry when she left and so she would have to sneak away from her. After washing her face in the bathroom, Maria brought the baby downstairs.

47

"Can you bring her into the kitchen?" she asked.

Tapiwa was still engrossed in watching TV.

"Tapiwa?"

"She is all right," he said, waving his hand at her.

Maria sighed and made her way towards the door.

The baby put her arms up and cried out for her.

She closed the front door to an outburst from Chichi and the sound of Tapiwa telling her to shush. Maria's stomach tightened as she walked to the bus stop.

She worked in Stevenage as a care-staff member at Blue Pines Home. She ordinarily rode the bus because Tapiwa rarely drove her to work. There was little to do during the early hours of the afternoon shifts because by that time the residents had been bathed and fed.

After Amy, the Jamaican carer, handed over the notes to Maria, she sat in the living room downstairs with the three residents. There was Kate Morrison who was in her early twenties. Kate had cerebral palsy. Then there was Richard Morton who was in his early forties but looked much younger. Richard was severely disabled and wheelchair-bound. He had a tendency to randomly lash out at objects, sometimes even hurting himself. The third resident was Sally Brown who was beautiful save for her deformed legs. Sally was also wheelchair-bound, but her mental disability was not too severe, although she had a habit of repeating sentences. Maria had seen flashes of normalcy in Sally's face. She looked at Maria closely now and smiled. Maria returned the smile. Sally was Maria's favourite resident.

Hearing a car pull up outside, she looked out of the window and saw Nancy, a fellow Zimbabwean, parking her lemon-green Audi. They had come to England at the same time. Late again, Maria thought, annoyance creasing her brow.

Nancy, who was dressed in a red frilly blouse and sky-blue pair of denim shorts, waddled in, wiping sweat from her face. She smiled at Maria and her face creased. She sat in a chair, her bottom extending over the seat, breathing heavily. "Hi, Maria. *Uri*— are you okay?"

"Am okay."

"I am late. Traffic jams. Getting worse. It is hell."

Maria kept quiet. Nancy picked up a handover sheet and read about the residents' condition from that morning. She sighed and pushed the sheet away. "Did you read the story about the ox-drawn ambulances, Maria?" she asked, laughing.

"I did. There is no hope for Zimbabwe."

"Soon, old Bob himself will be driven by oxen," Nancy laughed, slapping her fat thighs.

"It is sad. I am happy I came here."

"How do you chase white farmers from the country just like that? Zimbabwe will soon be like any other African country," Nancy said, steadying Richard who had started hitting the side of his wheelchair vigorously.

"Old Bob thinks war veterans are better than white farmers to run the farms," Maria said.

"How is Tapiwa?" Nancy asked, changing the subject.

"Grumpy as ever," Maria answered.

"Hmmmm. That one will never change." Nancy said, grabbing a gardening magazine.

"I thought Britain would change him, but it seems to be making him worse. Maybe it is the odd jobs he is doing and the cold weather that make him so ill-tempered," Maria said.

"Does he still beat you?" Nancy asked, half-mocking, as if blaming Maria for letting herself be beaten.

Maria clenched her fist and stroked Sally's hair. She glanced at her watch. Time was moving fast now.

"I have just remembered," said Nancy, standing up, "we need to cut vegetables for supper. Let's move the three to the kitchen." As the two women worked, they chatted. They heard the two care-staff members upstairs moving things. They were also preparing supper for the four service users.

After work, Nancy, who lived in St Albans, gave Maria a lift back to Hatfield. On the way, Nancy said she needed to stop by the home of a friend who was throwing a party in Welwyn Garden City.

"Oh but I must get back," said Maria, thinking of Chichi.

"It will only take a few minutes," said Nancy.

Maria's heart sank as they arrived at the party which was already teeming with people.

A huge Zimbabwean flag hung at the entrance of the open gate. Maria gazed at it and was overwhelmed by a flood of memories of home. She remembered her grandmother who was a *svikiro*, who read futures and had once told her when she was young that she would only attain happiness after great suffering.

Maria had never forgotten those words. They nestled within her like a virus. When would her happiness come? When would the suffering be over?

The din at the party was overwhelming. Many partygoers were Zimbabweans who were with their wives or girlfriends, along with a few other Africans.

A large woman wearing a greasy apron was dishing out *mazondo* to party goers. All of the men were clasping canned beers labelled Carling, Carlsberg, Fosters, and Stella Artois.

Maria's heart started beating fast. She knew she would be late home and she had no plausible explanation to offer to her husband. A number of her old friends who had not met her for a long time were happy to see her. "*Makadii, makadii,*" they greeted her with hugs and kisses.

Nancy pulled her to an empty space near an old sprinkler that lay on the floor like a snake. They found an old bench near a pond whose murky water sent out a scent of mould.

"Let us have a drink!" said Nancy.

Maria tried to protest but Nancy had already wiggled away, pushing through the noisy crowd. A few minutes later she came back with two glasses of wine and offered one to her friend. Maria saw Nancy looking at her, a half-smile playing on her lips.

"You deserve it, yes?" said Nancy.

Maria took a sip and found the wine sweet and warming.

Nancy took a swig and urged her friend to drink. "Come on, Virgin Mary. Drink. Don't be afraid of that villager you call your husband." Nancy laughed, throwing her head backwards.

"We have to go, Nancy. I will be late."

"Late for what?"

"I know Chichi will be missing me."

"There is Tapiwa to take care of that. Let him look after her for once. He is full of shit. Look at the clothes you are wearing. Long dresses like you are a gogo."

"Keep quiet," Maria half shouted.

"I wish I had married that pig husband of yours. I would teach him a lesson on what it means to live in England. He is too much of a villager," Nancy said and laughed.

Despite her protests, Nancy gave Maria another glass of wine. Maria wanted to go home, but Nancy insisted they stay a little bit longer.

"One more drink," she said. "Then I will take you straight home."

Maria had tasted wine before when they took residents out for dinner on special occasions. It was bitter and made her mouth churn, but she drank the glasses Nancy offered, feeling helplessly stuck but also, somewhere deep down, jittery and rebellious. By the time Maria and Nancy left the party, it was well past midnight. An uneasiness rose in Maria the nearer they got home. Tapiwa wouldn't be happy about her returning home so late.

Nancy dropped her at her house. "*Maita basa*," Maria thanked her friend and rushed inside.

She opened the door and found Tapiwa in the living room, watching a documentary on BBC Four on Somalia. Six empty cans of Stella Artois lay scattered on the floor. His eyes were raw and red. His face had a distant look, as if he could not easily see her. He turned off the TV and straightened himself to face Maria who was about to go upstairs.

"Where have you been all this time?" he demanded, forcing her to stop in her tracks.

"I was, I was…" she stammered.

"See, I have caught you. You whore!"

"But let me—"

"Let me what?" Tapiwa was moving towards her unsteadily. He swung a fist and caught Maria on her jaw, sending her staggering backwards into the wall. She made no effort to defend herself when he came at her again, raining blows on her face. She groaned and began to cough violently. Bending over, she vomited the wine onto the carpet and the foul smell filled the room. Tapiwa smelled the wine and went into a frenzy.

When he stopped, Maria lay motionless, feeling the blood pool under her skin. Her eyes were closed, and she heard Tapiwa leave and climb the stairs.

She remained curled on the floor, unable to move, unable to even put her hand to her face to touch the swelling she could feel building.

She drifted in and out of a looming, nightmarish sleep, still curled in the foetal position, and dreamt that her husband was creeping towards her with a hammer. In the dream she rushed to the kitchen and grabbed a knife. She turned and stabbed Tapiwa in the heart and twisted the knife. He fell to the ground, bleeding profusely.

She woke up to feel dried blood caked inside her nose.

That's it, she thought as she slowly began to move and lift herself off the floor. If she didn't do something now, he would kill her or she would kill him.

It was dawn. She heard water running in the bathroom. Tapiwa was bathing, readying himself for work. She held the wall as she stood and felt the pounding in her face. Her whole body ached, as though she'd been in a car accident. She went to Chichi's bedroom. The child was still sleeping peacefully.

All that commotion and still the child slept.

Thank God, she thought. Thank God.

On the way to the main bedroom, she met Tapiwa coming out of the bathroom.

53

"Here is the whore," he said, shaking water from his head into a towel.

"I am not a whore," she said quietly, staring solidly at him.

He seemed surprised at her boldness. "You did not tell me what kept you away last night. I wish I had not come to this bloody country. Everything here stinks," Tapiwa raved. "Look at the whoring going on here among our women. Look at the weather, the hard work, the racism."

"Why can't you go home to your country if you are fed up with England?" Maria brashly challenged him.

For a moment, Tapiwa stood looking at her. Then he turned and went into the bedroom, finished dressing and left the house. She heard the car start and drive off. In the bathroom she examined her face in the mirror and was shocked how swollen her eye sockets were and by the puffiness on her jawline and cheeks. Her hair stuck out in bunches.

She took a hot shower before going back to bed to try and rest. The pain kept waking her. When she heard Chichi coughing in her bedroom she went to her door and looked in. The child was rubbing her sleepy eyes.

Maria lifted her. Chichi looked at her mother and smiled, oblivious to her bruised face. Maria hugged Chichi close to her. "Chichi. We will be leaving this place soon," she said, kissing her on the cheek.

It was the first time she had ever said the words out loud.

And the first time she ever meant it.

"Where are we going, Mummy?" asked Chichi. Maria realised that Chichi probably thought the whole family would be moving out.

"I don't know yet, dear," she said.

The following Sunday, Maria left her husband watching a football match between Liverpool and Arsenal and took Chichi to the service at the Redeemed Church. The pews were full. The Nigerian minister, Pastor Nwanko, was preaching about goals in life.

"Don't live a targetless life like the gentiles," he exclaimed. "Ours is a spiritual journey, brothers and sisters, full of snares and traps. It is not for the weak-hearted. It is not by accident that we came here to England. Our God is above all obstacles in life. He is above racism. He is above the Home Office, which is always out to deport us. He is above failure, job losses, marital problems, financial problems. Fear the giant-mover, not the giant. God, Jehovah-Jireh, is our giant-mover. The problem with us, brothers and sisters, is that we fear Goliath and not David who slew him with a stone from the sling. We are like Peter, who looked at the storm instead of focusing his eyes on the Lord. What is your vision, my brother? What is your goal, my sister?"

He pranced up and down the stage, raising the emotions of the congregation with him. Maria remembered how God had answered her prayers before by enabling her to come to England, when she knew she needed to get out of Zimbabwe. Now, despite her misgivings about divorce, Maria had a second vision.

She closed her eyes and there before her was her grandmother. In her ears rang her grandmother's voice, a voice she had not heard in many years.

"Now is the time for happiness. Now is the time for happiness."

Outside the church, she felt light, like a new being. She imagined she felt like Saul when he turned to Paul on the road to Damascus. The scales of fear and ignorance had fallen from her eyes. She was now free, devoid of the fear that had held her captive in a loveless marriage. She had wasted ten long years loving a man who did not care for her feelings.

She had never confided fully to anyone about her sad existence. Even Nancy, who was her best friend, had only known half-truths about what she was enduring with her husband. True Christians considered *svikiros* the devil's agents. When she became a Christian, Maria had buried her grandmother's words, forgot about them, and dismissed them as fantasy. But now, as she recounted the injustices she had endured at the hands of her husband, she realised her grandmother had been right.

She had to leave Tapiwa.

The next morning, after Tapiwa had left for work, Maria gathered her and Chichi's clothes. She felt light and elated as she hurriedly packed the three large suitcases. When she had finished, she called a mini cab. The Muslim driver, wearing a skullcap, helped her to pack her suitcases into the boot. Chichi was skipping about in the driveway, happy at the prospect of moving house.

Maria looked around at the neighbouring houses as she locked the door. "Come on, Chichi, let's go!" she said to her daughter.

Maria pushed the bunch of keys through the letter slot and turned towards the mini cab. When the taxi pulled away, she didn't look back. She had found a refuge that had agreed to take them in, and from there, she would find where she was supposed to go.

As the taxi turned the corner, Maria thought about Tapiwa, how he would come home in a few hours, step on the keys she'd posted in their door and search the house for her and Chichi, wondering why his lunch wasn't ready. She couldn't help but smile.

The sound of a siren up ahead wailed and Chichi pointed and said, "Nee naw," as a neon ambulance zoomed past, lights flashing.

"Nee naw," said Maria.

Maria thought of her grandmother, of the sight of her on her deathbed, how she had refused to be taken to hospital by an ox-drawn ambulance.

She had been right to save her dignity.

And she had been right in the future she'd seen for Maria.

From now on, Maria swore to herself, she would listen to her heart, to her memory, to her visions. That is what would save them. That is how they would get by.

Mrs Skerman

I met Mrs Skerman through a dating agency. She was 20 years older than me (if I go by what she told me), but she looked much older. I've always found it hard to put an age to white women though.

The first thing I noticed was her pronounced ugliness. The skin on her face was thick and leathery, making her resemble a walrus. She had wrinkles around her eyes and a deep frown line in between her brows, as though a small axe had made its mark. She had a fleshy double chin with a beard sprouting from it, and though she shaved every morning, it never helped to smooth her complexion. The blade left ugly red marks which were worse than the beard. She was also unusually tall for a woman and walked with a shuffling gait, her meaty hips moving piston-like. She spoke in a halting voice that fell somewhere between a whisper and a growl.

I met her at a pub called The Mad Hog in East London. I paid £30 to the agency that arranged the meeting. It was the cheapest dating agency I could find. Others charged more.

I was dressed for the occasion in my best clothes: blue jeans, a white Che Guevara t-shirt and a black coat. I felt smart and hoped she'd liked what she'd see. I had to act fast before my visa expired.

The Mad Hog was full on the night. Though the lights were dim, I quickly observed that a number of women in the pub were old and ugly.

Mrs Skerman had described herself as a lonely, bubbly lady, wealthy and outgoing. She said she was looking for a young man from any cultural background.

After a few beers, she had still not arrived, so I started dancing alone on the dance floor. A number of women, some with partners, were also dancing. I saw one woman who looked like the Mock Turtle from Lewis Carroll's *Alice in Wonderland* sitting next to an elderly man with a handlebar moustache. She was talking loudly and laughing hysterically, revealing a row of sharp-looking teeth. The man was reserved and sipped his red wine from time to time. At the table adjacent to the Mock Turtle, an equally unattractive woman was wearing a purple dress. She moved repetitively, and her face twitched. She occasionally looked up from her glass of wine, her eyes blinking rapidly. At the far end, I saw two women who would have been at home at a freak show. One was almost a hunchback, the other cadaverously white like an albino. In fact, as I examined the other women, I realised all of them had one major defect or another.

The few better-looking ones had partners. As time went by, I was getting impatient, wondering if my date would come at all. When I was about to give up, a woman came through the door, scanned the place with intelligent eyes, and quickly headed in my direction. It was around midnight.

She extended her blubbery hand, introduced herself and pointed to a corner of the room. She ordered a beer for me and a Merlot for herself. She was dressed in a frilly chocolate brown skirt and a white blouse. She wore some expensive perfume that would have suited a better-looking woman. I could not stop thinking about how old she looked.

"You are from Ghana, Kofi, aren't you?" she said after settling down.

"Oh yes, I am from there."

"You were born on Friday—"

"Heh, how do you know," I asked drunkenly.

"I know. How long have you been in this country?"

I didn't like the question. It was reminiscent of being interviewed by someone from the Home Office. "I came a long time… a long time ago."

"How long?"

I ignored the question, lifting the pint to my mouth.

She asked me if I missed home. I shrugged. She looked at me straight in the eyes and I tried to concentrate on her stare but found my eyes were dancing. I felt it then. An understanding of sorts, that she might help me.

With so many beers in my belly, when she suggested dancing, I jumped up and led her to the dance floor. It was a slow beat. She held me close in a bear hug, our movements closer to body combat than ball dance. I repeatedly stepped on her shoes, but she didn't seem to notice. I felt we really looked funny, but the other people were too drunk to see. I found her more tolerable than the other satyrs in the room. Despite her unpleasant look, there was something charming about her. She was perceptive and seemed to understand human beings at a glance. When coupled with her ugliness, I found this disarming. Even now, I do not know if this is what made me get hooked on Mrs Skerman.

After that first night, we saw a good deal of each other, and when in bed, she climbed on top, I did not stop her. Before long, I moved in with her. We became what they call "partners" in Europe. We were quite a happy couple, apart from the shame I felt when I was out in public with her. I knew people in Europe married older women, but Mrs Skerman was fit to be my grandmother by any cultural standards. Whenever I went out with her, I was conscious of people staring at us, a young African male in his twenties with an old English woman.

Mrs Skerman seemed not to care what people thought. She sometimes kissed me in public, but I always felt embarrassed and failed to return her romantic overtures. Maybe I needed an acting course to enable me to show genuine emotions.

I still had to get around to persuading her to marry me before I could get rid of her. I had to do whatever it took to marry her and get a British passport. She called me Kofi while I called her by her given name, Jane. I would have been more comfortable calling her Grannie or Auntie.

The time I spent with her changed me greatly. I remember one hot day going out together. She was wearing a white skirt and a lime-coloured floral top that folded into the rolls of fat on her stomach. I wore short-shorts and a sky-blue muscle t-shirt that enhanced my physique. I was, however, not pleased with my black hairy legs protruding from the shorts.

Mrs Skerman seemed really proud, parading me in town. We crossed Hatfield Road and walked towards the town centre. I fell into a trot behind her since she walked very fast, as if she were furiously exercising. Hearing someone calling me, I turned back to see Mr Ampiah, a Ghanaian from home. He was large and black and worked as a bin man, a job that, back home, was for very low-class people. Only cattle herders were lower.

"How are you?" Mr Ampiah greeted me in Ashanti.

"Fine," I answered in English.

Mrs Skerman had stopped and was standing at a distance, waiting for me, an expression of disapproval at my time-wasting showing on her face.

Oblivious to this, Mr Ampiah continued talking. "Heh, man, you have a *Mami panyin* with you, heh?"

I ignored the question. *Mami panyin* was a derogatory word for old women in Ghana. He meant well, but he never knew how such comments affected me. "Sorry, I am busy, talk to you later," I said, moving away. I caught up with Mrs Skerman who had already moved on a good distance.

Even though I didn't mean it to happen, the years started to roll by with Mrs Skerman. Whenever I brought up the subject of marriage, she laughed, or changed the subject, or sometimes even got angry so that it became difficult to speak about it at all. I explained this to Kwame. He could not understand what stopped me from making her my wife.

I was comfortable living with Mrs Sherman. She had a large house that I helped clean. It was bright and airy and had a garden that needed weeding and mowing. I liked to feel useful. I felt like more than a house boy though. She held me when I slept and I liked the comfort of her round, warm body. I had long moved past the ugliness and was used to the pleasures we gave each other.

It was hard to push the issue of marriage when at home, we were, generally, happy. Yet I desperately needed to legitimise my stay in England. Kwame started doubting if I was really serious about marrying her.

Mrs Skerman had told me that she had been married once, but her cousin Ethel later told me that she had been married three times. She did not say to whom. Mrs Skerman had very few friends or relatives. Ethel, who lived in Stevenage, was the only relative who visited us occasionally.

Theirs was a love-hate relationship. I heard them row several times, and on those occasions, I would retire to the bedroom to let them resolve what I considered their family affairs.

Ethel was pleasantly fat with dimples in both cheeks. She was much more attractive than Mrs Sherman and kept her hair long and coloured. Whenever I caught her looking at me, I felt uncomfortable and exposed. Her eyes were steely like those of a cat.

One day, in the spring sunshine, Ethel came to visit. Mrs Sherman brought Ethel out to the garden where I had set up the summer tables and chairs. I served them tea and biscuits and retired to the living room to polish the bookshelves. Mrs Skerman worked as a psychologist, and it had made her rich. The living room was stacked with books on subjects like psychiatry and anthropology. The windows were open, and I could clearly see both women though I wasn't so much interested in what they were saying. However, when I heard my name mentioned, I immediately focused my attention on their voices. Back home, my mother had told me if you don't mention a person's name, you can talk about someone next to you and they would not know they were being discussed. Now, I was being discussed.

It was Ethel who had said my name, and crossing the room to be nearer the open window, I knelt down, pretending to polish the coffee table to better hear the conversation.

"Kofi, is he still trying to marry you?"

"Yes, but I have him at bay."

"You are mean to him."

"I am not mean, Ethel."

"How long can you string him along?"

"He's stayed this long."

"He's cleverer than you thought."

"Yes, he's not as simple as I thought, that's for sure."

"You like him."

"Yes. I do."

I stopped polishing and moved closer to the window, keeping out of sight.

Ethel laughed.

"You witch!" I could sense some genuine appreciation in Ethel's observation of her cousin's shrewdness and a tinge of jealousy in her voice. Mrs Skerman laughed heartily.

"I wish I had a toy boy," said Ethel.

After a minute Mrs Skerman said, "Let's go inside, it's getting chilly out here."

I rushed to the kitchen and started cleaning the fridge. I heard their heavy footsteps coming in. They entered the living room and paused to look at the aquarium. From the partially open kitchen door, I could see their backs crouched over the tank.

"Oh, poor thing. How old is she now?" Ethel asked, pointing at an orange fish which was the biggest in the tank.

"Ten years."

"Ten?"

"She was there when I was with Mike."

"Oh ... I remember."

Then Mrs Skerman turned sharply, as if suddenly remembering something. "Kofi dear! Are you there?"

"Coming, luv!" I called back, going to the living room at half-a-run-half-a-trot pace.

Ethel eyed me, but this time I was surprised that her usually steely look was replaced by a look of tenderness, of pity perhaps.

"What are we having for lunch, Kofi?" asked Mrs Skerman.

"Beef casserole and mash," I answered.

"Get going with it then. Ethel will be going soon. She needs to catch the train back to

Stevenage."

As I made the ladies' lunch, I thought how I would have to leave now and how I'd have to do it in secret. I couldn't tell Kwame, lest he start giving me advice. I felt sad and stupid that I had been taken in. I was satisfying the sexual fantasies of an old woman who could not find a white man to live with.

My chance came when one morning Mrs Skerman announced that she was going to Scotland for a three-day workshop. She was vague on what the workshop was about, but I assumed it had to do with her profession as a psychologist. I fussed over her, telling her how I would miss her. She said it did not matter since she would be phoning me daily. I drove her to Luton airport and returned to the house, feeling anxious. Once there, I packed my clothes in a bag and went to the safe where she kept her money. Mrs Skerman had long ago given me a bank card that I used for household shopping. She kept cash in a small safe in the bedroom, but I knew the code.

When I opened the safe, I saw a bundle of cash. It must have been thousands of pounds. To show that my departure had nothing to do with money, I took only £150 just to see me through the days I would be on my own before I settled down.

I got a biro and wrote on a piece of paper:

Dear Dr Jane Skerman,

Congratulations for keeping me this long. I heard your garden conversation with your cousin Ethel. Time has come for me to move on. Thanks for your 'kindness.' You have won in keeping me this long. We were both living a lie: me staying for my own selfish reasons and you keeping me for company and whatever fantasies you harboured. I won't give you my address and don't expect to hear from me.
*   (Formerly) Yours,*
*   Kofi*

I taped the note on the bedroom door and picked up my bag. As I was about to go out, I heard a car and went to the window. Peering through the bedroom curtains, I saw it was Ethel. What the hell did she want? I was annoyed that my plan to leave now would be delayed.

I tore down the note from the bedroom door and then went down to the front door and let her in.

"Ah Kofi? You are here!" she said.

She was wearing make-up and her hair hung down around her face. She looked the nicest I had ever seen her. To my shock, she closed the door behind her and lunged forward towards me, kissing me on the mouth. The perfume she wore filled my nostrils. I could also smell beer on her breath.

She stopped kissing me, grinned and went to the kitchen where she took two lagers out of the fridge. She handed the beer to me and drank hers from the can.

"All alone eh?" she said.

I nodded.

"My African prince. You will be lonely without Jane, won't you?"

I nodded again and shyly sipped my beer.

"Are you all right?" she asked.

"Yeah," I said, but my heart was racing. I was confused. Never had I expected such an advance from Ethel.

She came over to me and clasped me with her right hand, still holding the can with the other. I wanted to protest, but the feeling that overwhelmed me got the best of me. She noticed the bulge in my trousers and laughed heartily, throwing her head back.

"My Mandingo. Always ready," she said.

Putting down her beer, she started kissing me violently. We kissed in the kitchen, in the hall, and made our way to Mrs Skerman's bedroom. I thought about the note in my pocket, folded, the Sellotape still attached.

Afterwards, in bed, we both lay on our pillows, looking at the ceiling.

"She won't marry you," said Ethel. "You know that?"

I said nothing.

She turned to look at me.

Feeling her steely cat eyes boring into me, I turned to her and stared back.

"I will," she said, rubbing my face. "I'll do it."

Back home there is a proverb that says: Don't think of tomorrow because tomorrow will sort itself out. I smiled and let her kiss me, and I smelled her perfume in my nose.

Till a Snake Shows Its Venom

Obi Akwari sat on the beach looking at the setting sun, his massive frame filling the reclining camp chair. His sagging belly covered the better part of the Bermuda shorts. The sun loomed big on the horizon, a giant beach ball. He was too far away in his thoughts to be bothered by the din of the children yelling, playing football in the sand.

Since his wife, Grace, had passed away a decade ago, Obi had felt old and lonely. To fill his time, he walked Palaver, his Pekingese dog, in the morning and turned his attention to writing in the afternoon. He had been writing essays on the need for the Igbos of Eastern Nigeria to secede from the rest of the country. In his work, he was not only targeting Nigerians, but the Western world as his audience, especially the Britons and the French, who were responsible for the genocide against the Igbos during the Biafra civil war during the late '60s and early '70s.

Protesting had been part of Obi's personality since he was a young child. He'd understood that the only way to get something you wanted was to shout about it and refuse to back down. It drove his mother crazy, and she had often beaten him when he refused to do something she wanted him to do. It had never worked. Obi never, ever, gave in.

In his writings, Obi blamed himself and the other activists for not holding the Britons and French accountable. Each afternoon, his hands went into a frenzy as he typed on the purple HP laptop he'd bought second hand from a college student on Gumtree. The 'E' key had worn away. His essays could fill a tome. Change was coming. He was sure of it.

Obi's children, who were scattered all over Europe, had stopped visiting him regularly. They had all come when he suffered his first stroke shortly after Grace died, but when he'd suffered two more strokes after that, only Ihuoma, his youngest, had made the journey home. Now on his birthday, cards arrived from across Europe with elaborate, loving poems published by unknown poets. The cards featured golf sets, cars, and often, whiskey bottles. Obi had never drunk alcohol in his life, nor had he experienced the pleasure of a golf green. He wished his children lived near him and could visit.

His phone rang – the ringtone was the opening notes of the Biafran national anthem – and he fished it from his shirt breast pocket. It was Ihuoma, calling from Switzerland. She was his only daughter among his six children. His heart rose in his chest with joy.

"How are you, Dad?"

"I am alright. How are things, Ihu?"

He tried to keep his voice light. He wanted to appear upbeat and pleasant, to keep her on the phone as long as possible.

"Arrested again Dad! I saw the picture."

Obi laughed loudly. He chuckled as Ihuoma sighed loudly down the phone.

"Daaaaaaaaaddddd," she said.

"I am targeting the creators of Nigeria," Obi said. "These are the consequences."

"Please, Dad, it is time you stopped this protesting business. It is going to kill you."

"I can't stop," said Obi, serious in his tone now. "If I stop, then who will call for reparation?"

"I understand, Dad, but you can still write about all that. You just don't need to go out on the street... getting arrested. I mean at your age—"

"There is no effective way other than—"

"I am just worried Dad."

Obi went silent. A child called out as he tripped and fell head first into the sand, chasing after a football.

"I know," Obi said. "I know Ihu."

When he hung up the phone after promising his daughter that he would try to take it easy, Obi slumped back into the camp chair. Despite his fatigue, he could not sleep. Last night, he had written until he passed out. This book would be called *The Parallel Between the Holocaust and the Biafran Genocide*. It was possibly his finest work to date. Every Igbo should know that the killing of millions of their tribesmen was a result of an imperial international conspiracy that put profit before people, especially the lives of Africans. They should realise that successive Nigerian governments, especially the Northern-dominated military regimes, had long tried to push the Biafran genocide into the archives of history. Other tribes in Nigeria, including southerners who shared a common religion of Christianity and similar cultural practices, were wary of the Igbo's superior business acumen and academic brilliance which could only be likened to that of the Jews, who, like the Igbos, were hated because of their success.

He would bring this parallel to the world. He wanted Nigerians and the public at large to know that Igbos had suffered and continued to suffer the same atrocities that had been meted out against the Jews during Hitler's Nazi regime. The entire world had once lent their support to the Jewish effort to alleviate bigotry and the pain of the horrendous abuses that so often accompanied it, so why not do the same in defence of the Igbos?

All of this had been in his mind as he had worked at his desk last night. He didn't remember falling asleep, but he'd woken around 2 a.m., his head resting on the computer table.

As he sat on the beach now, he remembered Grace and tears came to his eyes. Their bond had been more than husband and wife. He didn't like the word 'soulmate' which is what people had bandied about after she had died, but he supposed it reflected something of what they'd had. He wondered if he would meet her again in the afterlife. The Christians talked of the righteous being reborn with new bodies in heaven. He'd been born a Catholic, but as he grew older and educated himself, he'd found his faith slipping away. Still, he had enjoyed the rituals. As an altar boy he'd loved the smell of incense and had hid his chuckles behind his hand at Father O'Brien's sermons. The priest's mispronunciation of Igbo words sounded obscene to the native speakers, but the priest had never worked out what he was doing wrong.

Obi had been baptised John. He had tried out the word on his tongue many times as he had grown up and always disliked how it sat in his jaw. When he attended school, they'd had to fill out forms which asked for their Christian names, as if their vernacular names were pagan. His father encouraged him to be a good Christian, but when he was killed, Obi found it hard to understand why God had allowed it to happen. Obi had later gone to his mother and asked how could God exist? His mother had reprimanded him and asked him to pray for forgiveness. When he told her there was no point, his mother said he was pig-headed

71

and ignorant. But Obi did not feel ignorant. He felt he was awakening. As his anger festered, the urge to protest grew inside him.

A beach ball hit the side of his chair. He looked up and saw the white child to whom the ball belonged come running towards him. Picking it up, he threw it back to the boy. He had quite a good arm – he used to play soccer in the Nsukka Eleven when he was studying for his BA in English Literature at the University of Nsukka, shortly after the Biafran war broke out. He'd been young and energetic then. He'd boxed, too. Some of his colleagues had called him the Nsukka Dick Tiger because he'd won all his fights.

The boy stared for a moment before turning to run off. It irritated Obi. Why could the boy not say thanks? What sort of manners were children taught these days?

It was time to leave. He got up and packed up his chair with a loud snap. He left the beach, shaking the sand from his sandals, his face a grimace as the thoughts of all the injustices he had faced in his life ran through his head. If Grace were with him now she would have seen his face and said "Don't be so grumpy, old man."

When he met Grace at the University of Nsukka, she was pursuing her BA in History. She'd been a shy young woman from Lagos. Grace's father, Mr Nwanko, was a well-to-do businessman who had been the first Nigerian to open a pharmacy in Lagos. Obi's father was a mere school teacher who taught in Kano. She'd had smooth, chocolate-dark skin and a gap between her front teeth that Obi found beautiful. They had dated for a year and a half before he proposed marriage, a lengthy courtship, which was very un-African. People were understanding, however, since the two were educated and many considered them to be encompassing the ways of the whites whose customs, including their education, had until then been treated with suspicion.

Grace had agreed to marry Obi after consultations with her rich and proud relatives, many of whom were opposed to the match on account of Obi's lack of wealth and status. The tribal and regional factors worked to his advantage however, when it was discovered that their parents came from the same village.

When Obi and Grace graduated, they got married, and while they had planned on taking a honeymoon, the civil war broke out. Ojukwu Odumegwu declared the secession of the republic of Biafra from Nigeria, something that would define both their futures.

There was much jubilation among Igbos who, all along, had been intimidated by the Northerners who accused them of trying to dominate other Nigerians, an accusation Obi found unfounded. His parents had attempted to go back to Eastern Nigeria when the persecution and killings of Igbos started in the North.

When word came that his father had been caught up in the slaughter, hacked to death with a machete, his head completely severed from his body, Obi had fallen to his knees. According to what Obi learned from his mother, his father had been identified by his pursuers who had ordered him out of a mammy wagon with the words "Only God Knows". She herself had escaped death at the last minute when one of the assailants had told the murderers to spare women so that they could tell the story of the massacres to intimidate other Igbos. A week later, Grace's father had been burnt alive in his car in Kaduna where he had taken supplies for his shop.

"Only God Knows," Obi repeated the mantra to himself as he came to terms with the fact that he would never see his father again. The memories of his mother's cries for her husband never left him. "*Chineke! Chineke!* Why have you forsaken me and taken my beloved one?" His mother could not be consoled.

As Obi made his way towards the bus stop, he carried his chair with some discomfort. His arms were still strong, but his back and hips were weakening and walking any distance caused him great pain. He searched for a bench to take his weight for a few moments. As he sat on a cold stone seat, worn with rain and littered with discarded cigarette ends, he thought about the strength he used to have. How had it evaporated like steam?

His latest protest, the one that Ihuoma had just called him about, had left him in bed for two days afterwards. Standing outside 10 Downing Street with his placard had pushed deep pain into his bones. He'd had to take tablets when he got home to try and ease the stiffness in his joints and when they didn't help, he had been forced to find a GP who could give him a script for stronger pills. Today he had come to the beach in the hope that the sun and sea air would ease his pain.

He had worn his best executive suit for his protest with one placard reading: "*Britain should own up for the Biafran Genocide*". The suit separated him from being associated with the other protesters, some of whom looked like tramps. He wanted to be taken seriously. He had always dressed like a gentleman for his protests.

It had been a sunny day, the sky cloudless, a pristine sheet of blue. He held another placard aloft, printed with the words "Britain and Biafra" in dripping blood-red. The top part of the poster depicted a skeletally thin child, an image that had dominated the British Press during the Biafra conflict. He knew that many Britons remembered it. In his other hand, he held a megaphone and, shouting into it at the top of his voice, had accused the Britons of having double standards in their approach to handling the world's injustices. He accused them of being part of the allied forces, together with Russians and Americans, in defeating the Biafrans. He protested for six hours before he was arrested and taken away.

During his protest, a stringer photographer had captured an image of Obi, with the megaphone in his hand and his placard high above his head. With the sun glinting behind, the photo had been quite breath-taking when it appeared in a national newspaper. The sun behind had resulted in a halo effect of light, highlighting Obi's sombre face and the message on his placard.

When the BBC picked up the story for its "Focus on Africa" show, Obi received a call and felt his heartbeat rise in his chest as a producer interviewed him in detail. At the end of the call, the producer asked if he would appear on the show to discuss the topic. Yesterday morning, he had taken a taxi to BBC studios and walked in the door in his executive protest suit. He was taken to a make-up room where he had his face blushed with powder and his shoulders dusted down. When it was time, he was taken from the green room and asked to perch on a sofa in front of the presenter and the nation of Britain.

"The nation of Biafra ceased to exist in 1970," said the presenter, introducing their item, "lasting only a mere four years. Now, one man, Doctor Obi Akwari is comparing the genocide of the Igbos to that of the Jews during the Holocaust. Dr. Akwari, you're very welcome."

Obi gave a brief smile before launching into the topic that had taken over his mind and soul since he was a boy. He spoke of his fears that Nigeria could never unite completely considering the deep-rooted ethnic and religious tensions created by the haphazard way the country was formed. He told of his disenchantment with the lukewarm approach of other Igbos to bring the perpetrators of the genocide to account. He said the Movement for the Actualisation of the Sovereign State of Biafra (MASSOB) was not radical enough for his liking.

The presenter nodded and asked probing questions, allowing Obi to delve deep into his political opinion, which, due to his daily writing, came out in measured, logical sentences. At the end of the interview, the presenter smiled and said she thought it was a topic that deserved further discussion and perhaps he would like to come back another time to do so.

"Anytime," he answered, like a seasoned politician.

When Obi and Grace had arrived in England, Obi applied and was accepted for a Masters in English at the University of London. He went on to do his PhD while Grace supported them as a nurse, having left her history education behind. Times had not been easy, especially after Grace had got pregnant with their twins Akuada and Chike, but when he had graduated, Obi had secured a well-paying lecturing job that meant Grace could give up nursing completely.

The more he studied academically, the more Obi became aware of the injustices laid upon the Igbo people, not just at the hands of the perpetrators themselves but the other nations who had let it happen. In university in London, he grew tired of thinking. He was going to do something about his thoughts; he was going to act.

One night he announced to his friends his intentions to stage his first protest. They were seated in the Pig's Head in their favourite corner, a haunt populated by students who brought in their own alcohol to mix with the soft drinks they bought there. Obi didn't drink, but he enjoyed the conversation. They christened their corner the Arena, likening themselves to Greeks who would debate issues in the public forum. He had been sporting an afro, a look shared by many university radicals then. James Brown had just released the protest song "Say it Loud – I'm Black and I'm Proud". The slogan Black Power, coined by Stokely Carmichael, was printed on buildings, t-shirts, and even guitars.

His friend, Tim, who was from Trinidad and had come to England to study economics, was wearing a leather jacket and a beret. His long hair made him look like Che Guevara. He was a member of the Black Communist Party and wrote some protest poetry. Ikenna was wearing an African tunic and spotted sideburns. Obi liked Ikenna's discussions, but he considered him more of a theorist than a pragmatist. He was like several University lecturers at Nsukka who theorised a lot but did not participate actively to champion the Biafran cause. They were nicknamed Sabos. Nkem had been wearing a suit and spoke with a forced English accent.

"What's happening in South Africa, comrades, is criminal," Tim said, lifting a pint of Guinness to his mouth. "I thought the world had learnt by now from America that the fucking colour bar bloody thing can never work in this century. It is bloody impractical."

"That is only part of the problem, Tim," Nkem said. "Blacks should also learn that the best way to fight the white man is to develop themselves and be his equal in technology and science. Look at the Japanese—"

"Bullshit!" Ikenna cut in. "This is a white-dominated world. The former colonialists were selfish and would not allow themselves to be on a par with Africans if you consider the fact that the whites control the world."

"No, Ikenna, you have got it wrong. What I mean is—"

"I know what you mean, Nkem, the white man should continue working with former colonials, keeping tabs on their development, making sure they are qualified according to their standards before allowing them to take another step." Ikenna's expression reflected his disgust.

"You guys need to agree. That's why the all-damn Pan-African thing ain't working at all. Them black comrades are busy fighting each other," Tim said, laughing.

Obi looked at Tim. "Before we talk of Pan-Africanism, we have to sort out our national and regional issues. These guys know about the Biafra genocide, and here they are talking about other countries—"

"But we have to—"

Obi didn't let Tim finish. "No. Look, I understand what you're saying, but before we consider others, we have to look at ourselves as Africans. As Africans we have nations and tribes. What I'm saying is we should desist from talking so much. It is time to act." Obi struck the table with his fist, adding emphasis.

Ikenna locked Obi's gaze. "There are so many causes. What cause are you championing?"

"The Biafran cause. And I am doing that practically. Not merely talking in pubs about the problem of blacks."

"How?" Ikenna spread his arms, a wide gesture of unbelief mixed with derision.

"You ask me how. I will disrupt the Nigerian independence celebration next week just to bring awareness to what happened to Biafrans."

A silence fell. Nkem and Ikenna looked at each other.

Tim adjusted his beret. "That will be revolutionary, man."

"Practically revolutionary," Obi had added firmly.

And so, true to his word, Obi made his way to the residence of the Nigerian High Commissioner in London where he had been invited as a guest. The new High Commissioner, Muhammad Suleiman, had just been appointed and Nigeria was celebrating her eleventh year of independence. He was a short man with tribal marks and carried himself with the self-assurance of a head teacher. He was dressed in an overflowing green and white *agbada*, representing the national colours of Nigeria, and he smiled broadly as he shook hands with some of the people in the audience. His wife was equally flamboyantly dressed in similar colours, complete with a headdress. She was a matronly woman who beamed at the gathering and seemed to be at home with the protocol. Green and white balloons, sponsored by Western Union, flapped in the cool October England wind. The balloons were emblazoned with golden letters which read: Happy 11th Nigerian independence, "Out of Many, We are One".

The commissioner was yet to deliver his speech. Nigerians and a few Africans from other countries were mingling, evidently enjoying themselves. Nigerian foods like garri and egusi soup were on display along with drinks from home like Nigerian Guinness, Nigerian Fanta and malt drinks. Someone in a car a few yards from the gathering was playing King Sunny Ade's "Moti Mo" on full blast. The announcer stood on a raised platform in front of the microphone and tapped it with his fingers, producing a "bup" sound. He called for order and stated that the High Commissioner was about to make his address. He asked everyone to stand up to sing the national anthem.

Obi Akwari watched the man who was operating the music system. In his jacket, he had a small tape deck which he'd placed on the inside pocket of his jacket. It was snug and heavy against his breast. The announcer adjusted the microphone to accommodate the commissioner's shorter height. The commissioner stepped to the podium, clutching a batch of papers in his hands. After saluting all the dignitaries and the assembled crowd, he began reading his speech. He talked of the recent peace in Nigeria and the improving economy which was a clear sign that Nigeria would soon be the envy of Africa and set an example of what good governance should be.

The commissioner's audience looked bored as though they had heard these words numerous times. Everyone wanted him to finish his speech so that the real party could start. The commissioner coughed asthmatically and continued with his assertion that Nigeria would soon be the superpower of Africa. In the heat, the balloons were wilting. From the back of the room, one let out a slow hiss. When the commissioner bent to pick up a glass of water, creating a brief silence, Obi took out the tape deck from his jacket pocket and pressed the play button. The initial notes of the Biafra national anthem rang out. As he sang along to the first stanza, the commissioner paused his speech, hunting for the source of the disturbance. The audience followed suit, looking around uneasily. Obi walked through the crowd and mounted the dais, his voice gaining confidence, even rising in triumph as, surprisingly, no one challenged him:

Hail to Biafra, consecrated nation,
Oh fatherland, this be our solemn pledge:
Defending thee shall be a dedication,
Spilling our blood we'll count a privilege;
The waving standard which emboldens the free
Shall always be our flag of liberty.

Two hefty security men went for him. Obi shouted: "Long live Biafra! Long live the Land of the Rising Sun!"

While one guard grabbed the tape recorder, the other one wrestled him to the ground, cuffing his hands before yanking him back onto his feet. Before they dragged him off, Obi jerked his head in the commissioner's direction, shouting, "That man is a liar! He is the one you should arrest, not me!"

He was quickly whisked away, protesting and yelling at his apprehenders. He was bundled into a car and at the police station, he had identified himself as Doctor Obi Akwari of the University of London. After being detained for two hours in the cells, he'd been released without charge.

Back home, Grace, who was equally committed to the Biafran cause, had scolded him for his actions. He had been sitting on the sofa, having removed his shirt for his wife to rub Vaseline on the bruises on his back and face.

"Obi, it is getting out of hand. You won't achieve anything by protesting with placards and songs about Biafra," his wife complained.

"I don't just do it to get the attention of Nigerians, I also do it against the Britons."

"I know, Obi… I know."

"I will not rest until I publicise what happened to my people, so that the Nigerian government owns up to their involvement in the genocide. Look at the Jews. They have succeeded in bringing to book the people who were responsible for the Holocaust. What is wrong with trying to punish the perpetrators of the genocide against the Igbos? If we keep quiet, people will think we are cowards. The Igbos say that unless a snake shows its venom, little children will use it for tying firewood."

"But the same Igbos say that a mature eagle feather will always remain spotless," his wife had replied as she had capped the Vaseline and handed him his shirt.

Despite her admonishments, Obi had gone on to cause a subsequent commotion at three more Nigerian independence celebrations and several other official Nigerian gatherings. The Nigerian embassy eventually banned him from attending any of their events.

Things got worse. His party, the Biafra Front, had been banned in Nigeria, and the leftist and underground newspaper *The Biafran* had been closed down. Its editor, Mr John Ugbedor, had been arrested and charged with preaching tribalism with a view to secession. There was a cartoon in one national newspaper depicting him as a tribal chief. Mr Ugbedor had succeeded though in disseminating information in Eastern Nigeria that all Biafran children should be taught what happened during the genocide as part of the regional curriculum. After the banning of the party and its newspaper, Obi had decided to change his strategy by targeting both Nigerians and the British.

Sitting on the stone bench, with his camp chair beside him, Obi thought how getting on to television had been the highlight of his protests so far. All his years of thinking, talking, writing and risking arrest had come to this point. He realised he'd made mistakes in his early strategies to bring awareness to the plight of his people. He understood why his daughter was worried.

As the sun disappeared below the horizon now, Obi shivered slightly and got up to leave. His phone rang, the Biafran anthem shrill against the evening atmosphere. Obi sat back down to answer it and was surprised to see his son's name flash up. Chike never called. He was the worst of all his sons for keeping in contact.

"My boy," said Obi, answering the phone. Then a thought struck him. Was something wrong? Had something happened to his son or his wife or their daughter, Lulu?

"Dad!" said Chike. "You've been busy. Have you seen the news? I can't believe it, eh?" Obi sat and watched buses, cars and cyclists pass as Chike told him to go home and put on a news channel immediately.

Obi's protest and BBC report had been picked up worldwide. There were protests at universities in several parts of Eastern Nigeria. Street names had been ripped off and handwritten wooden signs replaced with names remembering fallen heroes of the Biafra secessionists, names like Christopher Okigbo Road, Emmanuel Ifeajuna Road, and even Half a Rising Sun Road put in their place. The picture of half a rising sun was pasted on many public institutions in Eastern Nigeria. A Nigerian rap star called Soza Boy had set the Biafran national anthem to rap. Though the song was immediately banned, it was being played among the youth in Lagos and many parts of Eastern Nigeria like Enugu.

"You've gone viral Dad," said Chike laughing. "How did that happen, eh?

"Oh," said Obi calmly, tears gathering in the corners of his eyes, "Only God Knows. Only God knows."

A Dream Deferred

"What happens to a dream deferred?
　　Does it dry up
　　like a raisin in the sun?
　　Or fester like a sore–
　　And then run?
　　Does it stink like rotten meat?
　　Or crust and sugar over–
　　like a syrupy sweet?

　　Maybe it just sags
　　like a heavy load.

　　Or does it explode?"

'Harlem' also known as '**A Dream Deferred**'"
By Langston Hughes

Shingi heard Mrs Johnson talking to her Alsatian dog, Tarzan. He had somehow become used to these nocturnal verbal outpourings. When he first came to work for the white family in Eastlea many years ago, he found it strange for a human being to talk to an animal so emotionally. He knew that back home, one talked to an ox to make the animal move faster. The kind of verbal exchange he heard between Mrs Johnson and her dog was nothing like that.

Even when Jackson, the Nyasa gardener who had worked for the Johnsons for many years, explained to him the strange ways of the whites towards their animals, the way they called them human names, spent money on little coats, tied the hair above a dog's eyes in a bow, he still could not comprehend the behaviour.

Shingi remembered a story he had heard when he came to Salisbury from Zvimba. A black man had been shot dead for kicking a white man's dog. The dog had attacked the African's five-year-old son, and the child's father had merely kicked the dog to get it off the poor boy. The white man had got a gun and killed the African father without much reflection or second thought. The incident had led to protests by natives and forced the authorities to pass the Dangerous Dog Act. But the white man had got off with nothing more than a fine when his lawyer explained to the court how attached his client had been to the pet, how "he treated the dog like a child."

Now, recalling the story, Shingi wondered about the child whose father had been shot. How had he fared in life, without a father? Where was the boy now?

Shingi could not sleep. A rivulet of sweat trickled down his face. His body felt sticky and, rising onto his knees, he opened the window. He heard cicadas and the faint jangle of a police siren echoing in the distance. The sound was a reminder of who owned the land now, that only a few years ago, blacks had claimed as theirs. Shingi cupped his hands over the windowsill, breathing in the fresh air that stirred through the small room assigned to him in the servants' quarters. No bigger than a closet, it contained only a rickety wooden bed and a chair. There were a few old newspapers which he liked to read in his spare time. Mr Johnson had encouraged him to read so he could improve his English. The white newspapers were full of stories about parties, fairs, picnics, and concerts.

Mrs Johnson's voice got higher and more emotional. Her bedroom, near the servant's quarters, was open, giving Shingi a clear view of his mistress as she poured her heart out to poor Tarzan. Since the death of Mr Johnson a year ago, she had been acting strangely. She shouted more loudly at her servants and forgot to pay them until reminded. She had become cruel and short tempered.

Tarzan wagged his bushy tail and barked at some unseen object outside the window while his forelegs pawed at the window pane. Mrs Johnson pulled him back and gripped him tight. The dog wriggled, his ears erect and ready as if he were guarding the world's most valued treasure.

Picking up a folded old newspaper, Shingi fanned himself. He suppressed the urge to cough. In the glare from the lights, Mrs Johnson looked even more gaunt and pale than she did in daylight. Although she was in her fifties and wrinkled, her face had the attraction of a much younger woman. The maroon night dress she was wearing shimmered, and her lanky frame towered over the dog even in a seated position. She turned the restless dog to face her, grasping the long hair on his head to steady him.

"Oh my good Lord, he is gone. Gone, gone… It feels like yesterday. Do you know how I feel, Tarzan?" Mrs Johnson stared into the dog's eyes. The dog gazed back at her, as if in amazement, reminding Shingi of the dog he had seen on the His Master's Voice gramophone.

Loyal.

And obedient.

Mrs Johnson released her fierce grip on the dog to find a handkerchief to wipe tears from her eyes. "I know you understand, Tarzan. You know for sure how I feel, don't you? I never offended Dave, no, not one single day."

Released, the dog jumped off the bed and onto the floor. He ran under the chair in the corner of Mrs Johnson's room. Mrs Johnson buried her head in her sinewy hands and cried even more hysterically.

Shingi lit a cigarette and drew at it as if sucking traditional beer through a straw. He saw Mrs Johnson stand up, still muttering to herself, but this time he could not hear what she was saying. *Strange woman*, he thought as he took another drag from his cigarette. *Talking to a dog. Why can't she find a man to replace her dead husband?* Shingi remembered Mr Johnson as a quiet man who had left the role of house maintenance to his fault-finding wife. Yet, whenever he had intervened to protect a servant from her, he'd always succeeded. The servants had loved him for this, though he was usually taciturn. He sometimes went out with his Winchester shotgun hunting birds. He brought home his prey in a sack. Shingi often watched as he shook out the dead feathered things on the veranda to show Mrs. Johnson. Tiny bee-eaters, sparrows and wood doves. Lapwings, tinkerbirds and once, a fluffy-looking owl.

Mrs Johnson would smile and clap her hands. She plucked the feathers she liked for her hats.

Mr Johnson had been a stocky man with a pleasant sunburn. He'd worn khaki shorts and spotless white shirts. He would sit in his rocking chair, smoking a pipe while reading a newspaper. He spoke a smattering of Shona and Ndebele. He was the only white man Shingi had ever known who addressed blacks by their original names, though he pronounced Shingi's name as "Shing." The other whites, including Mrs Johnson, called their servants "John," "boy" or "girl." It was always "Boy, do this," "John, don't do that," or "John, you are a lazy kaffir."

A mosquito entered the room and buzzed around Shingi's forehead. He swatted at it, but missed, then moments later, feeling a tingling pain in his calf, he swatted at the insect again, only to miss it once more. He spotted it, flying clumsily, fattened by his blood. Back home, they used a special type of wood to drive away mosquitoes. The strategy seemed simple, but it worked as well as, if not better than, all the fancy sprays in the world.

Memories of home flooded him with a wave of nostalgia. Hot nights always had that effect. He especially found himself remembering his father, Choso, who had died almost a decade earlier. Choso had worked for several whites before he retired home. One white man had given him nothing but a watch after twenty years of service. Another had always complained he was a lazy, cheeky kaffir and had eventually chased him from the farm, paying him nothing at all. His father had walked with a limp, had bloodshot eyes, and ruled his household with an iron fist

It was only Shingi's late mother, Ma Shingi, the oldest wife among Choso's harem, who could tame him. She seemed to understand the source of his bitterness. The other *maininis* feared him and ran away whenever he lost his temper, which happened quite often.

Shingi remembered how his father had beaten his youngest wife, Ma Chido, for spending too much time at a church meeting. Ma Chido's maiden name was Grace, but she was called by her son's name, Chido. She had been forced into an early marriage and had to drop out of school at standard two. She secretly spoke of going to Salisbury to join her aunt who wanted her to continue her education using the night-school programmes available to natives.

On that day of the beating, Shingi had been sitting in his hut, which he had built when he turned seventeen. His father had bullied him into building it, arguing that it was not good for him to live in the main house at his age. "During our time, we weaned ourselves from our parents even before our things started frothing. You good-for-nothing youths of today continue suckling even when you get married," he had chided.

Shingi was sitting inside the hut eating sadza with *derere* relish when he heard heavy footsteps outside striding at a quick pace. His father's large figure emerged into Shingi's view, carrying a log that could have dislocated the shoulder of a lesser man. His shadow passed Shingi, leaving a smell of snuff and sweat. Shingi quickly finished his meal and stowed the plates.

He was afraid to go outside for fear of being reprimanded by his father. He was supposed to be cultivating the maize field but had chosen to roof his leaking house instead, a task easier than the backbreaking job of tilling the land with a hoe. From the corner of his eyes, he saw his father drop the log at Ma Chido's hut and head in his direction, his skimpy, once-white shirt hanging loosely on his bulky body.

Here it comes, thought Shingi.

"Where is Ma Chido?" his father asked.

"Gone to church," Shingi answered, relieved that his father was directing his attention elsewhere.

"Church, church. This church business is getting out of hand. What these blacks see in a white God and a white Jesus I don't know." He shook his head and spread his palms sideways before turning to walk back to the main house. Shingi heard him sniffing his snuff and coughing asthmatically.

Shingi went outside and heard singing from the path that led to the well. Three women wearing *chitenge* wrappers appeared. Ma Chido was among them, leading them in a Shona song they had just learned at church. She sang in a beautiful and lilting voice, a song that was about escaping this world to a place where there was no suffering:

I am going home;
It could be today, tomorrow, anytime;
I am going home;
I am tired of this wicked world;
O Sweet Jesus take me home,
For I am weary.
O Sweet Jesus take me home.

People talked about Ma Chido, usually pitying her because Choso beat her all the time, and many people feared for her health. Shingi also felt she was too young to be married to such an old man. Choso was very possessive and lived in fear that she would leave him for a younger man. His jealousy clouded his moods and his judgement.

At least when Shingi's mother was still alive, Ma Chido had had a shoulder to lean on. The older wife felt for the younger woman and consoled her whenever their husband beat her. Ma Shingi knew how to stand the beatings, which she understood were part of being an African wife. Now that she was dead, Ma Chido had no one to confide in. A great rivalry and hatred divided the other two wives, who hated each other and Ma Chido.

"Ma Chido!" His father's voice was coarse. Angry. The women stopped singing mid-verse.

"Coming. Am coming," Ma Chido answered and trotted to the house, her rosary swinging around her slender neck. She was dark and smooth like a plum. She had just plaited her hair in a new fashion with mounds of braids standing beautifully on her head.

Shingi heard his father shouting, "How many times am I going to tell you that this church business is taking over your marriage. Are you married to the priest?"

"No."

"Then why are you always at church? Answer me. Today is not Sunday."

"I have some roles in the women's group."

"And those roles are more important than housekeeping?" his father pressed further.

"No, Father of Chido."

"From today, I don't want to see you anywhere near that damned church. Do you hear?"

"Yes, I do, my husband."

Shingi was not surprised to hear his father stop his wife from attending church. He had not encouraged any member of his large family to attend any services. His hate for whites and all their institutions was legendary. He had witnessed a confrontation between his father and a deputation from the church that had come to tell him about building a house for a priest. The deputation was led by Jeremiah, a bold and well-adjusted man who dressed like a townie in clean clothes. A cigarette perennially dangled from his lips and he wore his hat at a jaunty angle. He had worked in South Africa before returning home. Unlike Choso, Jeremiah spoke reverently of South Africa. He said the place had more trains and cars than Salisbury. Some villagers, Choso among them, said he had been a *tsotsi*.

"I tell you, you are wasting your time building a house for the black priests. It is these stupid black priests who are being used, together with black policemen and teachers, to kill our culture. I lived with a white man for a long time, and I understand all his tricks in cowing black people. He can't penetrate our society without using some fools among us to champion his causes. Oh yes, he uses fools like black priests, chiefs and policemen. He convinced Lobengula to sell our land. He uses blacks for whatever causes he wants to impose on us," Choso said.

"*Aiwa, aiwa*. You have got it wrong. These whites are not here to—"

"How well do you know whites?" Choso asked, pointing his finger at Jeremiah. "I worked for them for many years till my hair turned grey. It is you young fools who think they are gods to be worshipped."

"I also lived with whites. I worked in Joburg, Durban—"

"As a *spiv-ta*!" Choso shouted sarcastically.

"Was that your job when you lived in town?" asked Jeremiah.

"It is you who lived by robbing people."

"Did I rob your mother of her knickers?"

"What? How dare you insult my mother, you bastard," Choso said, glaring at his rival. "You have wool between those big ears of yours and not brains like me! You good for nothing imbecile," he shouted, saliva flying from his mouth.

"You would make a very good candidate for a policeman, or even as a white man's dog," said Jeremiah.

"You come here to insult me and my innocent dead mother. For what! For what!"

Unable to take anymore, Jeremiah stood up and headed for Choso, his fists clenched tightly. Several men grabbed him and held him back, calming him down by speaking his son's name, Nyasha. "*Aiwa*, don't fight Father of Nyasha. We are only having a friendly discussion."

"*Mhata yako*! I can break the other good leg if you think I am afraid of you. I don't fear you like the other villagers," Jeremiah shouted, but he was whisked away. He and Choso were always at loggerheads because both of them tried to outdo each other in reliving their experiences in town. Choso also suspected that Jeremiah was interested in Ma Chido.

One day, Shingi was called by his father, who had been bedridden for months. Shingi was reluctant to go. Someone had once told him that when a person was dying, their ancestors held court, unseen, around the deathbed. Shingi had dismissed the story until he'd felt a strange presence inside the house. He felt it then, as he entered to find his father groaning on his reed mat. Several bottles of traditional medicines, along with calabashes and gourds full of tonic and other strange paraphernalia, were nearby. The room reeked of decay.

"Shingi, is it you?" his father called out weakly. "Shingi, the drop of my own liquid... you know..." He was seized by spasms of coughing which racked his already worn body.

His father was a shadow of the man he'd once been. Shingi could number his ribs through the thin bed sheet. His body was wasting before them.

"People think I am bad," he said, hoarsely.

"Not everybody, Father. We love you as a family."

"No. I know they think I am a monster, but they don't know who I am. Inside I am a kind person. Only your mother knew me well before the ancestors called her home. I changed when I came into contact with *varungu*. I am

94

dying without understanding them. They have chosen not to understand us Africans. We cannot live together as brothers and sisters. Never! It is like mixing oil and water. I understand their cruelty and disregard for other races who are not white. Oh yes, yes, I do. I understand their hypocrisy. I worked for this white man, Mr Cook. No, Mr Cook was my first one, then Mr Petersen."

He paused, seeming confused, and then his expression brightened. "Oh, I remember it was Mr Van Meer. Yes, yes. I worked for him for many years, and when I grew old, he chased me like a dog, giving me only a small amount of money. And when I complained, he threatened to call police to have me arrested. I dared him to do it. He said I was a cheeky kaffir and hit me with a sjambok. That's how my leg got broken. I felt it snap, just like that. And still he hit me, over and over, bam, bam! I called out to my ancestors; I thought I was dying. And then after, when I'd crawled away, he called the police and lied, saying that *I* had tried to kill *him*! And after hospital they put me in prison. When I came out, I had no *chitupa* to stay in town..." He broke off coughing.

Shingi listened to the terrible noise. It sounded as though his father's lungs were filled with fluid, like he was drowning.

"I came back here with your mother and your elder sister, Rambanai," he continued. "I could not walk properly, but with my handicap, I managed to start life afresh. I am telling you this not only because I am bitter about what happened, but because I have seen the same streak of violence and rebellion in you. Outside, you look humble, a characteristic you inherited from your mother, but inside you have my character, that of a stubborn person with a streak of

95

violence, which you try to suppress. I have seen this on your face and in your eyes when I am shouting at you. I know you can obey orders, but you do it with scorn that masks rage. I have always stopped you from going to work in town. I am now granting you permission to go. Promise me one thing, though, that you will be obedient to whites. I am not saying this because I am a coward, but because I have had enough experience to realise the powers they wield over Africans. Africans like policemen, priests, clerks and even houseboys, who work for them, attain this mysterious power." He stared at Shingi, his expression soft now, and with pleading eyes, lowered his voice almost to a whisper. "Always say things that will please them. They are like children; you can fool them easily. But don't try to be clever and challenge their authority. They can sense rebellion."

Shingi could see that this speech was sapping what was left of his father's strength, but he understood, finally, why his father hated the whites so vehemently.

His father reached out and, taking Shingi's face in his hands, he spat into it in a traditional blessing, then lay back on his mat, exhausted by the effort. Shingi tried to open his mouth to speak, but his father dismissed him with a wave of his bony hand, and he left the room with tears welling in his eyes.

Two days later his father was dead.

The household and harem that he had kept together fell apart fairly quickly. Ma Chido eloped with Jeremiah to Salisbury, taking her daughter with her. Of the other *maininis*, Ma Tapiwa went to live with her mother in Chitungwiza, while Ma Farai inherited the oxen and started to till the land. Shingi waited for a month before leaving for

Salisbury to look for a job. He had only gone up to Standard Two but felt maybe he could find something to do in town.

In Salisbury, Shingi bumped into Ma Chido and found out that Jeremiah had abandoned her shortly after arriving in Salisbury. He had been in and out of prison, and by the time Shingi arrived in Salisbury, Jeremiah had been convicted again for burglary and was serving a lengthy sentence. To keep herself, Ma Chido sold *chikokiana*, a local traditional brew. Shingi had also seen her several times in shady places, like Mapitikoti Beerhall, where she hung out with other women who indulged in casual sex. She'd aged since he'd last seen her too, and she now looked haggard, a shadow of her former beautiful self.

***

The memories of his home in the village that Shingi had pushed to the back of his mind saddened him. He had worked for the Johnsons for many years without any serious incident. As his father had advised, he had masked his anger by working hard, cushioning himself from the countless injustices he faced. Now Mr Johnson was dead, and he was trapped with his cantankerous wife who treated her servants like mules. The memories of his village brought everything into a new perspective, mixing both nostalgia with the bitterness of his experiences. At night he dreamt of home. By day, it felt as though his skin was bristling, as if something deep inside him was about to break out.

Shingi woke late the following morning and rushed to have a quick shower. He'd been regular about bathing ever since Mrs Johnson had told him to his face that he stank. Jackson, the older Nyasa gardener, had shown him how to wash properly. "It's not like back home where you just put water on your body. Concentrate here and here," he had said, pointing to his groin and armpits and showing him how to lather the soap up to a good foam.

Shingi put on his uniform, a pair of white shorts and shirt to match. He remembered something else Jackson had told him, that the white Master's dogs did not like dirty black people. At first he had not believed him, but he remembered a dog chasing him one time after he had missed his weekly bath. Or was it just a coincidence?

From time to time, the Johnsons sent him to deliver letters in the neighbourhood. Some whites set the dogs on him till someone from the house would identify him. Then the usual apology would be offered: "Oh, it is Mr Johnson's kaffir. *Basopo*, boy, be careful. The dog thinks natives are thieves."

He found Mrs Johnson already awake, reading *The Salisbury Times,* which was delivered to her door every morning. Meeting his glance, he saw that she had deep dark shadows under her eyes and looked tired.

"You are late again, John! But that is typical of you people!" She looked at her watch and grimaced.

"Sorry, Madam."

She only stared hard at him. There was hate and contempt in her eyes.

He went to the kitchen and started cleaning the breakfast plates. He then swept the house carefully, dusting all the nooks. He saw Jackson cutting the hedge. Jackson lived in the location like Beatrice, the laundry woman.

Tarzan came out of the bedroom, wagging his tail, and rushed into the kitchen, sniffing at Shingi's legs. Mrs Johnson, who had gone into the bedroom, came out.

Calling to the dog, she took him out to walk along the Jacaranda trees. Watching his mistress, whose shoulders were held high, almost to her ears, Shingi could not understand why she was so angry.

Beatrice carried in a giant bag full of washed clothes. Her face was bathed in sweat. She was almost the same age as Mrs Johnson, yet she was called "girl." She had worked for the Johnsons for many years. She boasted of sending all her four children to school single-handedly since her husband had left for South Africa and never returned. She now had one daughter in school.

"*Masikati*," she greeted Shingi, putting down the load with a sigh.

"*Masikati*," Shingi replied, wiping the bookshelf.

"How is our queen today?"

"Grumpy as ever. Gone out to walk the dog."

"Ha. These *varungu* and their dogs."

"I heard her talking to him last night."

"Is that news to you?"

"No, it's more the way she does it, so emotionally."

A silence fell.

Beatrice broke it: "How is your wife, Shingi?"

"I haven't been to the location yet. I hope she is fine. Our good queen won't allow me to go out."

"Don't stay away too long now that she is expecting. She must be due soon?" Beatrice winked roguishly. Shingi had been given regular time off on Saturdays to see his wife while Mr Johnson was alive, but nowadays he was afraid to ask the mistress for such a privilege.

Beatrice hauled another load of laundry outside, and Shingi was about to return to his room when he remembered he had not cleaned Tarzan's basket. Retrieving it from where Mrs Johnson had left it outside her bedroom, he went into the yard and he cleaned it using a wet cloth, working furiously. Jackson joined Beatrice in the yard. She worked diligently; her fat cheek pasted to her right shoulder, her hands deep in the tub.

After Shingi had returned the dog's basket to the house, he joined the two in the yard.

"Heh, Shingi," Beatrice said, "tell this Nyasa how expensive Ndebele women are. He has no cattle to pay *lobola*, and yet he thinks because he has a thing dangling in his trousers, he can get me the way you buy matches from Nagarji or CT Stores."

Jackson looked at Shingi, his wide mouth twitching with a mischievous smile. Clearly, he was expecting a favourable comment in return.

"Give him a chance," Shingi said, waving dramatically at Jackson.

"You heard that. You heard that, Beatrice!" Jackson jumped up with a triumphant shout. Going to his knees now, he looked into her eyes. "Please, Beatrice, give me a chance."

"*Voetsek*!" Beatrice laughed, splashing Jackson with soap suds, wetting his blue overalls.

Shingi laughed, his lanky body shaking.

Unbeknown to the three, Mrs Johnson was standing arms akimbo, a wry smile on her face. Tarzan was wagging his tail and his tongue hung out.

Shingi was the first to see her, and he went still. The others, following his glance, froze too.

"Is this what you are paid for? Clowning around like the wooden-headed kaffir you are?"

100

"Finished cutting the hedge, madam," Jackson said, toeing the ground. He looked more frightened than ashamed.

"And you, boy. Is this the kitchen?" she asked Shingi.

Shingi looked at the ground.

"I will cut what I pay both of you," she said as she walked away.

Shingi was horrified because he knew she never made empty threats. He needed money to buy napkins for the baby. A cut from his already paltry salary would crush them. As Jackson moved the ladder behind the house, Shingi went quickly into the kitchen and started washing plates that he had already cleaned. He heard Mrs Johnson muttering as she came in the door. A cacophony of clattering metal filled the kitchen. Shingi turned around to see the cutlery drawer in Mrs Johson's hands. She'd upended all the cutlery onto the floor and, having tossed the drawer aside, was now bent over the pile, separating out the spoons, forks and knives. She mumbled as she counted.

"What do they need cutlery for? They use their dirty hands to eat. Girl!"

Shingi watched, sensing an implosion coming. White people's dogs have names, he thought, but blacks are just "boy" or "girl." *We don't even deserve names.*

Beatrice came into the house, rubbing her hands against her cotton dress. Mrs Johnson pointed at the cutlery on the floor. Beatrice looked at the utensils, saucer eyed. Mrs Johnson kept her gaze locked on the black woman. The silence lengthened, becoming awkward.

"Some of the cutlery is missing." Mrs Johnson spoke sharply.

"I don't know anything about any cutlery," said Beatrice.

101

"Of course you do."

"I am not lying, I swear!" Beatrice passed her right forefinger over her neck in a traditional swear.

Mrs. Johnson ignored her. "And since I can't keep a thief here, leave right now!"

"Please, Madam, I have a daughter who is still in school—" Beatrice began.

"You should have thought of her before stealing from me."

"Oh *mai we!*"

Mrs. Johnson retrieved a purse from the kitchen shelf and, plucking out a crisp five-pound note, threw it to the ground. "Here!"

"You owe me more than that, Mrs Johnson." Beatrice was crying now, her big body shaking. She swiped at the tears with the back of her hand.

Shingi felt a lump of anger crawl into his throat.

"That is it. Go!" Mrs. Johnson pointed at the door.

Beatrice bent down and picked up the money and, broken-voiced, bid Shingi farewell with her eyes.

He acknowledged her with a stiff nod. His glance shifted to Mrs Johnson, and on encountering her stare that clearly said "get back to work," he turned from her and plunged his hands into the boiling washing up water, holding them there till the hot coal of his rage abated and all he could feel was the scorch on his skin.

***

It had been two weeks since Beatrice had been fired. Shingi worked mechanically, keeping his thoughts focused on his wife and the baby that was due any time. Today was

Saturday, the day Mr Johnson had usually allowed him to go home to see his wife. But those days were gone, and he knew it, the same as he knew he couldn't continue working without a break. The same as he knew that Mrs Johnson was looking for a chance to fire him. He wouldn't give her one, although his fury over his hopeless state warmed his blood.

He was tossing and turning at night. In the speckled mirror in the hall, his eyes were bloodshot. Sometimes he looked down and saw that both his fists were clenched.

He retired to his room for lunch after finishing his morning shift. He did not feel hungry though he had taken some bread and beef from the kitchen. He showered and retired to bed for a siesta. He had extra work to do in the evening: Mrs Johnson had told him she was expecting visitors.

It was later in the afternoon when the yellow Austin Morris roared into view, raising a plume of red dust. The visitors were Mr Haddock and his wife. They lived in Mabelreign and were among the first farmers to have settled in the area. The rickety car cackled and groaned before stopping. Mr Haddock reversed, sticking his right elbow and head out of the window, looking for a parking space. He ran over some red flowers and finally parked under an avocado tree. Mrs Johnson, who was standing on her veranda, watching, looked on expressionlessly.

Shingi waited nearby in case he was needed to give a hand. Since the sacking of Beatrice, he had more work to do now that there was no one to attend to the cooking or laundry. Seeing Mr Haddock raised a sand of aggravation inside him. Years back, the farmer had murdered a native and only been fined thirty pounds for the offence. In retaliation, another farmer, a native, had poisoned a dozen of Mr Haddock's cattle and run away to Mozambique.

Now, Mr Haddock struggled to get out of the car, carrying a cane. He was dressed in a khaki safari suit that was so tight, his rotund body seemed ready to burst forth. He was sweating profusely and continually wiped sweat from his red face with a dirty handkerchief as he waddled inside the house. Mrs Johnson and his svelte wife, who wore a broad hat too big for her head, trailed behind.

Shingi followed the group inside and started serving drinks. Whisky for Mr Haddock, wine for his wife, while Mrs Johnson settled for soda.

"Your kaffir has grown, Ethel." Mr. Haddock said, looking Shingi up and down. He squatted on a sofa, panting, his squinty eyes nearly closed. "Bloody piccaninny when I first came here."

Shingi stood erect, his face not betraying any emotion. But when Mrs Haddock looked at him sympathetically, he acknowledged her kindness with a smile.

"I don't like your kaffir, Ethel," Mr Haddock said, his hand outstretched to take the glass of Whisky Shingi offered. "Just look at him. He is the dangerous type. I have lived with these people and I know it."

"Stop it, Phil!" Mrs Haddock nudged her husband. "How on earth do you know he is dangerous?"

"He looks shifty, like a caged beast."

"Dave was attached to him," Mrs. Johnson said. "I couldn't understand what he liked in him. Poor Dave, he loved natives."

Shingi clenched his teeth.

Mrs Haddock sipped her wine. Mr Haddock drained his glass and heaved himself from the sofa to pour another glass of Whisky, dismissing Shingi's offer of help with a wave of the hand. He sat back down, gulped the liquor and closed his eyes tightly.

Mr Haddock continued to pour himself glass after glass of whiskey amidst protests from his wife. After the sixth glass, he started singing "For He's a Jolly Good Fellow." He sang drunkenly, tapping his foot on the floor. His wife paid him little attention, chatting instead with Mrs Johnson. Mrs Haddock spoke of her son who was in Australia and never wrote letters to his parents. She mentioned the bad knee that had prevented her from playing with her friends at the European Tennis Club. She then talked of the natives who were fighting for improved conditions for Africans.

Shingi heard Mrs Johnson talking about her late husband and how he had spoiled the servants. She said she planned to go to South Africa to join her sister who was in the textile business.

Despite understanding that this would mean losing his job, he felt somehow relieved.

Mr Haddock suddenly sprang to his feet and, grabbing his wife, swung her from side to side, yodelling a song whose words were inaudible. He spun her faster and faster until she freed herself from his grip. Throwing up his arms theatrically, he protested bitterly. But Mrs Johnson laughed, her blue eyes twinkling merrily. She looked very pleasant, Shingi thought, the way she'd often looked while her husband was alive.

A recollection of her recent cruelty to Beatrice and all the injustices he had suffered at her hands rose in his mind. He was so caught up in his resentment that he barely registered Mr Haddock's baleful stare before the man came for him in two long drunken strides and unleashed a punch, hitting him bang in the centre of his chest. Shingi staggered, feeling the pain shoot through his entire body. He felt a rage rise within him. It kept him upright, kept his hot stare fixed on Haddock.

"Stop admiring white women, kaffir!" the white man shouted.

"Leave him alone, Phil!" Mrs Haddock called.

Shingi stole a glance at Mrs Johnson. She kept her gaze averted from him and her mouth firmly closed.

Mr Haddock paid no attention to his wife and, doing a little jig, lashed out at Shingi again, putting all his weight behind the punch. This time, Shingi dodged him, forcing Mr Haddock to rush forward with the momentum and collapse against a cabinet, which wobbled on its legs. Regaining his balance quickly, Mr Haddock lunged at Shingi again, diving low and grabbing him by the legs. The two collapsed in a heap. Shingi's breath left him in a whoosh, and Mr Haddock, having an advantage, got up and began kicking Shingi on the ground. "Come on, kaffir," he shouted. "Fight!"

Shingi drew up his knees, struggling for air.

"Fight, kaffir!"

Shingi felt the force of the white man's boot drive into his ribs. Blows rained down. Shingi writhed in pain, but then rage came, muting his agony, fuelling him to his feet. He got up briskly, blood running down his face. He had done nothing wrong, but he knew of so many stories of whites beating Africans to death for no apparent reason. Wasn't Mr Haddock one of them? Hadn't he killed a black man without provocation before? Shingi locked his gaze on Haddock, and vowing it wouldn't happen to him, balled his fist. He remembered the admonition his father had given him on his sick bed. When the drunken man came at him yet again, Shingi felt himself punching the white man squarely between his eyes. It was like something possessed him to take that action. He felt pain shoot through his arm even as he watched Haddock fall, as if in slow motion, down, down, until his head struck the floor with a thud. He gurgled once and then there was silence.

The two women crossed the room and knelt beside him.

"He has killed him!" Mrs Johnson clasped her head with both hands. She'd turned pale and looked like she might faint.

With an effort, Mrs Haddock turned her husband onto his back, but there was no response. Collapsing over him, she cried, "Oh Phil, don't give up on me!"

Shingi stood as if rooted to the floor, speechless. He felt a sensation of triumph overwhelm him. He was another being, devoid of fear, devoid of the cowardice that had been part of him for so long. But within seconds, a voice from deep in his brain shouted at him to run, and he dashed from the room and out the back door. He could have easily defied that voice because he felt he had become a stronger person, but he had to see his wife before he was arrested.

He ran alongside two derelict barns, heading towards the white cemetery. It was the only deserted road he knew. This time of the night, police would stop any black man and ask for his *chitupa*. Especially one who was bleeding.

Pausing, he tried to stop the blood flow from his nose and the cut on his forehead with the hem of his shirt. The moment he resumed running along the railway line, heart pumping rapidly, he felt the flow anew, the blood trickling with his sweat. He felt faint, but he ran on. His bones ached, and his white shirt and shorts were soaked in blood. If he fell by the roadside, he knew he would be taken straight to the charge office before being attended to.

He avoided the main road that led to the white suburbs of Mabelreign, Eastlea, Greendale, and Borrowdale.

He could hear police sirens wailing in the distance.

The prisons were full of Africans who had been jailed for minor offences like looking at a policeman with what they termed a "scornful eye." Some were jailed for talking to a white man or woman while wearing a hat. Even using a white man's toilet was a serious crime.

Now, here he was, running away after killing a white man. He would surely be hanged. He thought of his wife and the baby, and he vowed to see her before they arrested him, although it seemed impossible in that moment, the distance home too great.

By now he was far away from the white suburbs and approaching Harare Kopje. He neared Arcadia across the Mukuvisi River on the right side of the railway line. A while later he approached the Harare African Township. Some educated black man who had studied in England had written an article in the now banned black newspaper, *The Chimurenga Tribune*, about racial divisions in Salisbury, using the railway line and the river as boundaries. As he ran parallel to the tracks, he realised how right the author had been. The railway and the river separated the races, confining them to different areas. The whites were on top, then the Indians, followed by the coloureds, and at the bottom of the hierarchy were blacks.

He stopped running and turned eastwards to the Old Bricks where he and his wife lived. Had she given birth yet?

Nine months had passed since she had become pregnant. He heard music from the locations and drunken singing from shebeens, where half-Christians, half-pagans sang both Christian and secular songs. He saw a man driving a mule-drawn wagon carrying excreta from the location. The man pulled down his cap as he passed Shingi, not wanting to be recognised. The hapless labourers who collected human waste were despised even by the lowest African. They did their work at night to avoid being identified. Children mocked them, and they were foul tempered enough that if they discovered which child had insulted them, and where they lived, they would take their revenge by emptying the bucket of human waste at the doorsteps of that house.

He knocked on the door lightly and stood back in the dark. His breath was shallow, his heartbeat anxious. Light from a candle glowed dimly from the window. He heard footsteps and saw the silhouette of a woman who appeared heavily pregnant. She coughed loudly and then called through the door, "Who is there?"

Shingi heard the shrill note of fear in her voice. "Who else do you think would knock at the door this time?" he asked her.

"Oh, is it you?" Now relief seemed to replace her panic. She opened the door.

He said, "If I was being chased, I could get killed just here at my doorstep."

She backed away, seeing the blood on his face and his soaked clothes. Walking past her, he sat on the bed. After recovering from her shock, she took off his bloody clothes and wiped his face with a dry cloth.

"*Mai-we, mai-we*. What happened? Oh my husband. Is it *tsotsi* who attacked you? You have blood all over your body."

"Get me some water!"

She rushed to the corner of the house and poured water into a basin from the bucket where they kept fresh drinking water and washed his face with another cloth, gently and slowly. Wincing in pain, he shrank from her touch. Once his wounds were tended, he lay on the bed. She joined him. He blew out the candle and pulled the sheets up to his waist.

"What happened?" she whispered.

"When nationalists say a white man is a dog, we should heed them."

"But you have always been against nationalists."

"Shut up. You want me to tell you what happened, and when I start talking, you interrupt me. What is wrong with you, woman?"

She fell silent, listening while he narrated what had happened until he said he had killed a white man, then she cried out, "God help us. You have killed a *murungu*!

"It was not intentional," Shingi answered.

"All the same. Killing a white man. Au! I would suggest you run away."

"Where to?

"Anywhere. Nyasaland, Northern Rhodesia."

"No."

"No, what?"

"I don't feel like running. Running away from what."

"Are you mad?" Sitting up, she stared down at him.

"I feel different… I mean I feel strong…"

"So, you want to hand yourself over, like a sheep before slaughter."

110

Shingi was silent. His wife started crying.

Then she said, "Oh, and who will look after my child if his father is hung for his actions? Oh, the world has no mercy." Despite his pain, her cries acted like some cruel lullaby, sending him to sleep. His wife whimpered until she too was quiet, curling against him.

They were woken by a loud knock early the following morning. By the time Shingi opened the door, a crowd had gathered outside. The sight of a Black Maria always attracted attention. Sergeant Dermott, who was well known in the location, was flanked by two black officers. The black officers wore khaki shorts and jumpers, brown boots and puttees wrapped around their legs.

Shingi was surprised at his resolve. He felt nothing. Time had stopped for him. It wasn't what he expected, considering the crime he had committed. If he felt anything, it was triumph, as if he had achieved something that had been crying for a solution. His wife followed him, and Shingi knew she was fighting tears.

Sergeant Dermott did not look hard like the rest of the white policemen. Shingi had heard that he had arrested more black people than other white officers. Shingi cast a glance over the crowd and saw an expression in their eyes similar to that which he had seen in the eyes of sheep back home whenever a dog was unleashed on them.

"Are you Shingi Chirenje, house boy for Mrs Johnson of Crested Crane farm?" the sergeant asked, his unflinching gaze locked on Shingi.

"Yes."

"Are you aware that you have killed a white man named Philip Haddock?"

"I am."

"Come with us to the charge office."

Shingi's hands were handcuffed behind his back before he was dumped in the Black Maria.

Another sensation gripped him when he thought how he had been addressed by his full name by a white man. He smiled and shouted, "I am Shingi Chirenje!" His voice was drowned by the crying of his wife.

"Don't take him," she begged. "It was all the white man's fault!"

Shingi watched the crowd disperse through the tiny window of the wagon. He saw his wife fade into the distance as it moved away, the dust rising, choking him.

As they left the Old Bricks behind, a large collie dog gave chase to the wagon. "Henry!" roared a voice. "Come back here! Henry!" Shingi peered through the slit of the window and watched as the black-and-white dog returned to its owners, a well-dressed white man and woman standing on the street. The man rubbed the dog behind its ears. The woman muttered something to the dog and patted its back. Shingi couldn't hear what she said but it looked as if she'd mouthed, "Good boy, Henry. Good boy."

The Hate that Hate Produced

Dear Reader,

I don't care who you are. You could be white or black, English or Irish, Hutu or Tutsi, Jew or Arab, Ibo or Hausa, believer or non-believer, or you could even be colourless. I really don't care. Whoever you are, I well know that you have not experienced what I have gone through. Your world is most probably a world of law and order. Mine has been a world where the impossible, the unexpected, takes centre stage. I have stopped caring for a world that does not care.

I have stopped worrying about conforming to societal norms because they are not more important than deviant behaviour. I see little difference between life and death, angels and demons, sanity and insanity, right and wrong, true belief and paganism.

I have killed, raped, maimed, and castrated. If I had not been granted asylum, I would have gone mad or taken my life. I thought I was safe by coming to England, but the woes I thought I had left behind have haunted me here too. Recently, I was diagnosed with HIV/AIDS. I know I got it from one of the numerous women I raped back home. My imminent death doesn't frighten me, though. I used to be afraid of dying when I was young, but not anymore.

I was brought up in the Roman Catholic Church, which had more rituals than those our ancestors used to follow. I was christened Peter by some red-faced white priest who poured water on my head and told me I was a new being. I only stopped going to church when I later realised the same Catholic white fathers who deafened our ears with the talk of a God of love and equality promoted the myth that Tutsis were superior to us. These idiots forwarded the so-called "Hamitic narrative" and its racist interpretation of Rwandan society. This narrative assumes that "Negroid" populations, from which Europeans claimed the Hutu descended, given their physical characteristics, were inferior to pastoral "Hamitic" groups of "Caucasoid" origin, distantly related to Europeans from which the Tutsis were believed to originate.

This racist interpretation – even if a less immediate factor in the historical analysis – set a fundamental premise for the 1994 genocide because it promoted and directed the internalisation of these notions in the country.

Well, the priest who baptised me could have been gay or a paedophile and yet his ilk regarded us as savages in need of salvation.

I have taken too many lives to fear death. I like that the Bible calls death "sleep", for that's what it is. Ecclesiastes talks of the meaninglessness of life, likening it to chasing the wind. Well, I have been chasing the wind for a long time. Many people are still chasing the wind and they don't know it. My wife, Gentile, says I talk in my sleep. When I ask her what I say, she tells me I shout to my tormentors to kill me.

Some of my friends who confessed to the Truth and Reconciliation Commission in those *gacaca* kangaroo courts apologised for the part they played in the killings. I pitied the poor fellows, because later, after enrolling for a part-time sociology course at the University of London, I learnt who largely contributed to the massacre. It was hypocrites like the ones who had convened the Commission. While they didn't initiate the bloodshed, they laid the foundation for the carnage to occur.

Unfortunately, these "Masters Of War", as one singer calls them, are the ones who have taken a judgemental stance against bringing peace between the two warring sides. They pride themselves in helping the refugees and offering asylum to former "butchers" like me.

The other day, I saw my name with several others from my tribe in an English tabloid. We were called Monsters, Angels of Death, Machete-wielders, Extremists, and Tribalists, among several other labels the western journalists have invented for our cursed lot. They said we were abusing the taxpayers' money. My surname was misspelt as "Nteyahananga" instead of "Ntuyahaga". This was a minor omission compared to the inaccuracies of the report about me. They said I work in Manchester as a cleaner and that I am a former *Interahamwe*. I work as a mental carer and I never joined the *Interahamwe*, though I took part in the genocide.

It is funny how these Western journalists and pedestrian analysts want to judge and classify us. Anyway, it is their world, and we are just people they discovered and conquered, the way Tutsis, who found us in Rwanda, lorded over us, castrating our chiefs to show their superiority.

Didn't we used to work for them during the serfdom called *ubuhake,* when we were required to give a portion of our yield to Tutsi lords in return for protection? They were our lords, like white colonialists who said Tutsis were lighter skinned and taller, a qualification that made them more well regarded than us broad-nosed and dark "Bantus". In colonial days, we were double victims of oppression from our own black kin as well as the white imperialists. Both groups treated us like chattel.

It is normal in history, though, for the conquerors to impose their values and attitudes on the conquered. The British did the same wherever they mounted the Union

Jack. The pioneers did the same to Indians in America and so did the whites in Australia, who classified the Aborigines among fauna and flora!

I am blaming the anthropologists, missionaries, historians and both Belgian and French colonial masters who said Tutsis were superior to Hutus and Twas. Those are the people I am condemning. Some anthropologists argued that Arabs, Ethiopians, Somalians and Tutsis were Hamites, far superior to us who, like our sub-Saharan counterparts, are Africans proper.

I had been experiencing the same judgemental attitude from my white workmates who only started addressing me as 'sir' when they saw a story with my picture in the newspapers. They now look at me with fear mixed with some strange respect borne of that fear and maybe even hate. Before that, I had been treated shabbily, like one who had run away from hunger and disease in Africa, which is one of the most insulted continents.

As I said, dear reader, I no longer care. Part of me has died. I am just surprised that after reading so many books about my tribe and continent, I have discovered that the people I thought were intervening to bring peace to my country are squarely guilty of what they, themselves, have labelled a tribal genocide.

While quoting the Ten Hutu commandments that called on my tribesmen to kill Tutsis, these perpetrators of half-truths and lies are not saying anything about the ten centimetres difference that was used to justify our inferiority to Tutsis. They are not quoting real monsters like Arthur de Gobineau, that colonial scholar who concluded that the physical differences between Hutus and Tutsis meant that we originated from different areas.

Maybe if it wasn't for foreign forces, the Rwandan genocide wouldn't have happened between us and our brothers, the Tutsis.

I have now realised the power that people who write have over those who do not. My history, even my future, has been defined by foreigners. I am writing a book to tell my own side of the story. It will be titled *The Hate that Hate Produced*. I am really tired of definitions and classifications that invent names like gentiles, Kaffirs, Osus, Niggers, Paddies, Pakis and machete wielders.

Yours,
Peter Ntuyahaga

Anna's Song

Hi Jane Njeri,

Jambo ndugu. I hope you are fine.

Can't believe five years have gone since you left. One of my friends said you were in Kisumu.

By the way, I have reconciled with my former husband, Mr Robinson. We meet from time to time, though we do not live together. I still use his name for prestige and for papers... you know.

Jane, I understand you are bitter for being deported, but I feel it is the Lord who saved you from this life of shame. The business is now hard for us old women. As you know, this *malaya* business is only good for young women.

The police are also clamping down on the trade, and many brothels have been closed. Oh you remember the Kenyan woman who used to run brothels in Soho, Mrs Osborne? Yes, Mrs Osborne; that is her name; the one who was married to some white man. She was caught, and her name appeared in all the newspapers. What surprised the *wazungus* was not her trade, which is not news here, but the money she made. Imagine, one million pounds!

I was in Manchester when I heard that you had been arrested and taken to the repatriation centre pending deportation. I prayed for you all night and cried like a child.

Jane... life is hard and strange... I thought I had escaped life in Majengo, but I have entered another Majengo that eats at your soul.

All the same, I have got used to life here. It is Africa that would be strange to me if I were to come back. How many years have I been here? I used to celebrate birthdays, but the last birthday made me realise that I have aged. I am 50! Just like that. Luckily, these *wazungus* are strange people. I have a few clients who like black flesh, even that of an old woman like me.

There is this old man, Father Sean O'Donoghue. He enjoys being whipped and cries out like a child, calling my name. "Do it, Anna, you black bitch! Whip me, bitch!" You can't believe what madness these white people have. And imagine this same man, conducting Mass on Sunday, using the same blasphemous mouth to say Ave Maria. Oh I wish God could strike him down with lightning, like He used to do in the Old Testament. I have never met a man who has such a dirty mouth. It is men like Father Sean who are delaying the coming of the Son of Man.

You remember the brothel called Dirty Dick in East London? We used to go there together... remember? There is this white man we have nicknamed "CCTV", who pays a fortune just to see women naked without sleeping with them. What happened last night when I went there was worse than what people used to do in Sodom and Gomorrah. If I had something else to do to make the kind of money I am making, I would stop what I am doing.

Some of my friends have stopped selling their bodies and are doing care work. I used to call care work dirty, but I am not the right person to call any work dirty because I have seen dirtier things in life. I pray for forgiveness. Is it not Jesus who forgave that prostitute in the Bible? I will write you later. Keep on praying and don't come back here. *Kwaheri ndugu.*

Yours,
Anna Gachiru

Dambudzo Marechera Writes to Samantha

Dear Samantha,

I think by now you have heard what happened when those hypocrites in administration chased me from their white university, giving me an option between being sectioned or expelled.

I chose the latter, a decision which shocked them out of their warped wits. I have forgiven them because, like you, they thought as an African student from some remote Southern African country, I was privileged for receiving tertiary education at Oxford, a learning institution they have overrated as a citadel of knowledge just like Cambridge or Harvard.

Such academic madhouses keep on churning out arrogant, snobbish, hypocritical and pea-brained bastards who enter the world with the superior airs of holier-than-thou 'we and them' attitudes, calling themselves 'Doctors', 'Professors' or any stupid titles to distance themselves from other ordinary folks whom they look down on as dunces.

These idiots have done little in changing the world into a better place. If anything, they have contributed to making it worse by joining their counterparts in the right-wing maggoty camp that influence policies that worsen this Babylon called earth. They wear gowns and mortarboards, receiving degrees from pink-faced old blokes who shake their hands and congratulate them for entering the world of knowledge.

I am glad I never attended the graduation ceremony at Oxford because I find that event nauseating. If I had, I vow

I would have dressed in my blue jeans with a T-shirt or overalls just to show how stupid the fucking ritual is.

I had the same experience at the University of Rhodesia, which was normally attended by middle-class white boys, when those white buffoons in administration kept telling us black students how lucky we were to receive education at the institution of high learning.

You always accused me of being strange, eccentric, bohemian or even mad. I can assure you that I am as sane as any bloke right-thinking people consider as being normal, whatever that means.

Do you remember the night you took me out on Valentine's Day or some other stupid social celebration at City Arms along Cowley Road in Oxford, and you kept on hanging on me and kissing me like we were movie stars? You were hysterical that I was not returning your love as you expected. The truth is, I am always annoyed when a white person starts showering too much love on me. I am less angry when you people are hostile against my race or even blatantly racist to the extent of calling me 'monkey.' I wouldn't fight back or take much offence as some blacks would do. A white person fawning over me never fails to arouse sleeping demons in me that are hypersensitive to hypocrisy, which I have been encountering since my childhood in Rusape after my father died.

I have had so much of this sympathising from white folks from my school days at the mission school and at Uni back home, when those hypocrites felt they were doing us a favour by civilising our cursed lot. I am almost paranoid when it comes to racism masquerading as colour blindness.

Remember how mad you became when I even rubbished the idea of marriage as another form of societal hypocrisy?

Well, I see no difference between marriage and fornication, whether one is sanctioned by some holy man claiming to represent God here on earth, or two horny fools deciding to copulate in the back of a car, on top of an office table or in some dark alley. Whenever I tried to explain to you things that have shaped my life, my childhood problem of stuttering nearly came back, scaring the shit out of me.

I have elected to write you this letter long after we have parted just to explain some of my views on life. I know I am anti-social, but most people readily classify me to be equally anti-freedom of an individual or even mad. I live outside their provincial world, just as I consider them outsiders in my world, which is hinged on freedom of an individual. The physical and mental insecurity that have dogged me since my father died have made me a stranger in a world where hypocrisy, lying and dishonesty reign supreme, making anybody calling the perpetrators of these vices broods of vipers, an odd one out or a dissident.

I have gone through several stages of identity crisis: self-hatred, self-re-examination, excessive afro-optimism, excessive afro-pessimism, reversal racism, escapism and alienation. Maybe it is a manifestation of these conflicting mental feelings that made the authorities at Oxford think of sectioning me.

After living rough in Oxford, where I pitched a tent near the Uni shortly after being expelled, I am hanging out a lot with my good Rasta friends in London. I am somehow in tune with these rootless, ganja-smoking pseudo-ideologists. We agree on many issues, like the world being Babylon – Western-influenced, materialistic, oppressive, manipulative and capitalistic. There is a lot of ganja and reggae music which I find soothing. I don't, however, agree with the far-fetched ideology of revering Haile Sellasie, that dictatorial midget in Ethiopia, as God. I also don't agree with their excessive promotion of blackness, which I find hypocritical and escapist.

Samantha, they say writers are show businessmen trying to interpret the world on paper, unlike their counterparts in music, who use music. There are two musicians I find interesting: Bob Marley and Jim Morrison. I connect with both of them in my lifestyle and telepathically. I feel both were shamans who died young and only received recognition when they were six feet under.

I have a premonition that I will die violently or young. I don't care because I don't feel I belong to this world. I am like an Abiku child in Yoruba mythology, a spirit child who is fated to a cycle of early death and rebirth to the same mother. Sometimes I dream of living in another age, where I was a griot who was burnt at a stake for lambasting some tyrannical chief. At other times, I dream that I lived as a poet who was drowned by the chief's henchmen for refusing to apologise for an insulting poem he had recited in a village arena against injustice.

Do you remember how Mrs Brown, our English writing lecturer, reacted when I wrote a short story on how I worked in a chief's palace, shaving the pubic hair of the women in a harem? I still remember the opening line of the story. It read: 'My job in Chief Molokolo's palace, the chief having all along thought I had been castrated, was to shave the pubic hair of his wives'. The story ended with me bedding some of his wives and paying the ultimate price of death. You remember how Mrs Brown blushed when I read the story aloud? She screamed that I was mad. Well, the morality of the story is that many leaders in power think their subjects are blind to their excesses in urinating on people's rights. They think we are castrated till we rise up and unmask their hypocrisy or demand for justice.

I might go back to Zimbabwe because I can't continue living like a tramp. I have already seen the inside of British Police cells twice or thrice. I have to finish the book I am writing first. It is called *House of Hunger*. I have destroyed several manuscripts of other books that I have attempted to write because I don't feel they capture the message I am trying to communicate.

However, as a citizen of the world, a polyglot, I feel going back home won't calm the demons in me that cry for a just society where the freedom of the individual is paramount. What I am reading in the Papers on independent Zimbabwe seems to be miles away from that ideal world, which both the repressive white regime of Smith and the popular nationalist black government of Mugabe are miles away from realising. Many African societies which benefited from the wind of change in the sixties have already failed to cut the umbilical cords of colonialism that connect them to their former masters both economically and socially. Nationalism might even be a guise of deep envy of the lives colonialists lived. I say this knowing that many African leaders just introduce follow-fashion-monkey societies that emulate the system they replace.

You see, Samantha, this thing called colonial mentality eats at the core of your heart or soul like a cancer. Many nationalists and even academics are irredeemable victims of colonialism, whether consciously or unconsciously. They don't realise how entrenched the problem is in their DNA makeup. They achieve what they call independence (from what?) and change flags and national anthems but fail to establish new home-grown societies based on their cultures, values and norms.

Many erroneously think achieving independence is the most difficult stage in attaining freedom. To the contrary, what is difficult is establishing a nation that is compatible with modernity. Every fool who has a healthy dick can impregnate a woman with no intention of having a baby. Raising a baby is the trickier part since you have to nurture the infant to young adulthood.

I know a number of my African intellectual friends who reject everything European in favour of everything African or black. These idiots need psychoanalysing by God himself since this is an extreme manifestation of self-hatred highly masked as race pride. Though I abhor most western practices, I am equally nauseated by most things African. The singer who sang "Say It Loud, I am Black and Proud" was in actual sense saying, "Say It fucking Loud, I am Black and Ashamed." Oh, yes, isn't it Louis Armstrong, hailing from the same shabby background, who honestly complained in song that his only sin was his skin?

Apart from my name, Dambudzo, I don't think, Samantha, you remember me revering Africanness or Blackness. Most whites are racists, including you and several so-called liberals, who shower us poor souls with love when they are consciously or unconsciously pitying us for being black. As I said earlier, Samantha, a white person expressing excessive love for a black person is simply saying you are also a human being, which is worse than any racist insult.

I remember my English teachers both at St Augustine's Mission School and the University of Rhodesia praising me for getting good results by saying, 'Well done, Charles. You are such a brilliant black boy'. A brilliant black boy? Fuck!

I could have killed those sons of bitches for not praising me because I was a brilliant pupil but a brilliant black boy. I know you would argue, Samantha, that I was being oversensitive, but what do you expect from someone whose race has received numerous insults since blacks and whites came into contact?

That's why even now, as I strive to establish myself as a writer, I don't want the title to go with the adjective 'black writer'. Fuck even other demeaning terms like 'black', 'Negro', 'coloured' or 'African.' A writer is just that, a fucking writer. Period. Knowing how condescending you are, just like many of your kind, you will quickly find a word in your language to define me. Strange, bizarre, eccentric, bohemian, unconventional, odd or even mad. It is your language. I wish I could describe whites in Shona – that is, use deep Shona, with idioms and proverbs that would elude even the most educated white linguist. However, I associate the language with backwardness, provincialism and squalor.

I might link up with you when I come back to Oxford. Meanwhile, I am still squatting with several friends.

Yours

Charles William Tambudzai Dambudzo Marechera

Sign of The Cross

With unsteady hands, Godwin Botha ripped the envelope open and removed the paper inside. Written on a page torn from an exercise book, was a letter from his wife. Her handwriting was scrawly but legible. Still, he drew nearer to the candle to read. Her news, that she would be joining him from Nyasaland in a week's time delighted him. He read the letter again, this time more slowly, to better savour its contents.

The silvery moon outside the open window was full and bathed the room in a soft, romantic light. His wife's letter made him miss his home in Nyasaland. He missed the lake and the people.

He missed his mother. Godwin looked through the window and up at the moon. His mother used to tell him a story when he was child, in his native *ci Tumbuka* language, about the moon. The moon had two wives, Navipyenge, who lived in the East, and Nazubulaninge, who lived in the West. Navipyenge, whose name meant "wait till the food is fully cooked", starved the husband whenever he visited her, and this explained why the moon was thin when it was in the East. The other wife, Nazubulaninge, whose name meant "you can taste the food even if it is not fully cooked", always gave her husband something to eat, explaining why the moon became fat when it was in the West.

Godwin smiled now at the memory. Africans still believed in such tales to explain phenomena they did not understand. He considered himself lucky to have received the white man's education at Livingstonia Mission. His father had sacrificed to send him to school, working hard at selling fish to raise money for Godwin's fees and upkeep. When he'd come home on holidays dressed in khaki shorts and shirt, he'd been the envy of the whole village. Upon graduating as a teacher, he went to Northern Rhodesia to teach at a school in Matero in Lusaka. Working as a teacher or a clerk was considered prestigious. With his first salary, he'd bought a Humber bicycle and a blue saucepan radio.

He sometimes went to Matero Welfare Hall to watch the bioscope show in the evenings. He paid three pennies for a ticket. He largely went there to while away the time, but he did not like the violent scenes that characterised the films. Many of them had the same theme: cowboy heroes facing brutish native outlaws whom they butchered mercilessly. Fights at the cinema were common because many in the audience wanted to enact what they had seen their heroes doing. A shout of "*Jeke! Jeke!* meant a fight was imminent.

He much preferred reading to watching movies and read voraciously to improve his English and to escape into the literature of far-away lands. He borrowed books from the library in the town centre or from his workmate, Mr Chanda, who had quite a collection of classics by writers like Daniel Defoe, Charles Dickens, Shakespeare (abridged) and Chekov.

He had been saving money to make the house look more homely for when his wife, whom he had recently married, arrived. From his savings, he bought more cutlery, bedding and several other household goods that he put away in the pantry. He did not want to use them in case they broke before his wife came in two months' time. The Indian shopkeeper gave him a pillow and a big pot as a bonus popularly known as *bonsela*.

Everything was going well until rumours of "vampire men" started circulating in the country, especially in Lusaka and on the Copperbelt. The stories linked anyone who had close association with white settlers or their way of life to be a "vampire man". Vampire men, locally called *Bamunyama*, were believed to be Africans who were employed by Europeans to capture people by touching them with a wand which rendered them invisible and helpless. Mr Chanda had warned Godwin that several parents feared African teachers at their school had been recruited by Whites and made into "vampire men" to ensnare pupils. He said the parents feared that their children would be made invisible and helpless, marked with the Sign of the Cross, and then taken off by the "vampire men".

This Saturday evening, when he was still cleaning the house in anticipation of his wife's visit, Mr Chanda picked up Godwin for a drink at the beer hall. The hall was teeming with people. It was month-end and many had money to spend. The hall had two sections, one for bottled beer and another section for opaque beer. The two friends sat in the bottled beer section at the corner, next to an open window. Godwin looked at the graffiti, which read: "We don't want Federation". Mr Chanda, who had gone to buy beers, came back from the counter with two bottled beers of Castle lager and placed them on the table.

Mr Chanda followed his friend's gaze and squinted to see clearly. He laughed out loud at the graffiti.

"These natives are being confused by Nkumbula. What do they know about Federation?" he said, leaning his cane against his knee.

"But don't you think the Federation is wrong?" said Godwin, taking a swig from the bottle.

"Natives should first go to school before they start talking about Federation."

"These are the seeds of nationalism," Godwin said.

Mr. Chanda ignored the comment.

The place was noisy and they had to shout to hear each other. Spokes Mashane blared from an unseen gramophone. On the opaque beer section, *tsotsis* leaned drunkenly against the walls, their hats askew, pretending to be cowboys. They spoke in a drawl with cigarettes dangling from their mouths. Most of them carried knives, and there had been stories of stabbings.

A couple nearby looked at each other, and the man said something about black men who were pretending to be white. The woman laughed and slapped her partner's thighs playfully. Both Godwin and Mr Chanda heard the comment.

"You know this talk about *Bamunyama*. We have to be very careful. I know these people and their superstitions," Mr Chanda said.

Godwin felt uncomfortable at the mention of *Bamunyama*. He had forgotten about the threat and all the talk of "vampire men"

"All African broadcasters, teachers and even priests have been branded *Bamunyama*," Mr Chanda continued.

"Why us?" Godwin asked.

"That I do not know," Mr Chanda said in a concerned and fatherly way. "I do not know if it is the hate for whites or the Federation that has brought about these stories."

"We should avoid going out in public," Godwin said. "We probably shouldn't be here."

"We are allowed to move freely like everybody else," Mr Chanda shouted in English.

The man who had commented about Africans pretending to be white coughed noisily, deliberately attracting attention. The woman laughed provocatively and pulled a face.

"Let's go outside," Mr Chanda said, standing up.

They went outside and sat on a bench against the wall. After they finished their beers, Godwin got them two more. They left the bar late, both feeling drunk. Godwin rarely drank and felt a slight headache.

After bidding farewell to Mr Chanda, he headed home to the Location. There, he sat in his sitting room, reading *The Pilgrim's Progress*. Down in the township, he could hear the beating of drums and people singing, probably coming from an illegal drinking den. Police made crackdowns on such places and local brews were confiscated.

He dozed off but was awakened by voices of men outside the window. His heart started beating heavily. He put the book away and listened. He saw two shadowy figures. One was tall and the other shorter.

"He is still awake. I can see the candlelight. These *Bamunyamas* don't sleep at night. They stay awake like witches," one voice said, sending a chill down Godwin's spine.

"Imagine such a young man employed to kill his own people. They are all *Kapulikonis*, these educated men. Did you see the bicycle he rides? It was bought from the money they give them to kill our people. Our children are not safe anymore," the other voice commented.

Godwin coughed noisily to announce his presence. The two men vanished into the dark. He closed the window and put the book away before lying on the bed.

The encounter was too close. Those men had been right outside his window. What if his wife had been here?

The following morning, he mounted his bicycle and rode the half a mile to school. Previously, people had shouted greetings like "How are you, *Mwalimu*". Or they had commented on his bicycle, expressing their admiration. He had felt important, as if he were a *Bwana Ndisii,* as the locals called the District Commissioner. But now people looked at him with contempt. He passed through Matero market, where some marketeers openly made nasty comments. "Here comes the *Kapulikoni*," one said. "These *Kamupilas* are so cheeky to ride a bicycle in public, daring us," said another.

Two men who repaired bicycles by a stall were busy at their work. They cast their eyes downwards, pretending to be busier than usual.

When he turned onto the small gravel road that led to the school, he heard people shouting, "*Kapulikoni*! *Kapulikoni*! *Kabulangeti*! *Munyama*! Go back to Nyasaland! We don't want killers here!"

At the school, he secured his bike to the rack, sweating despite the morning chill. The other teachers were waiting for him in the staff room. An impromptu meeting had been convened to discuss the accusations that had been levelled against them as *Bamunyamas*.

Mr Lubasi, the headmaster, was worried. He said wherever he went he was greeted with shouts of *Munyama* or Capricorn, with some people calling for him to go back to Barotseland where he hailed from. The Capricorn African Society was a pro-Federation organisation and it was a great insult to be called a Capricorn. Godwin shook his head and felt a knot in his stomach.

All day, the thought of the men at his window filled his mind. Now, they knew where he lived. He was in danger. If his wife came, she too was in danger. Should he tell her not to come? Should he write her a letter this evening?

When classes ended, he rode home, using a less crowded road. Later, as he prepared his evening meal, he turned the saucepan radio on, tuning it to the Central Broadcasting Corporation. The radio gave a cacophonous noise before tuning to a song by Alick Nkhata and Quartet. Alick sang about urban women who were imitating white women in fashion and behaviour.

Suddenly, he saw a Black Maria full of black policemen speed by. The Black Maria was followed by an ambulance. There was no political rally or Mbeni dances that he knew of, both of which usually attracted security men. Where were the police and ambulance going? As he peered out of the window, his neighbour, Mrs Gondwe, came to him with fear written on her face. Mrs Gondwe was a baker and visited him from time to time. She was his tribesperson and spoke to him in his native *ciTumbuka*. "Get out of this place till things cool down," she panted. "Your friend, Mr Chanda, has been beaten to death by a mob."

"Really! Oh my God. Why?" Godwin asked.

Mrs. Gondwe ignored his question. "One of the pupils at your school fainted at home, and his father, who is a neighbour to Mr Chanda, thought your friend had marked the boy with the sign of the cross. Several other teachers have been beaten badly. They did not get to you because you live too far."

Godwin thanked Mrs Gondwe and grabbed his few possessions, stuffing them in a cardboard suitcase. He looked at all the items he had bought for his wife. He could only carry a few items; he had to leave it all behind

"Go well, my son. Remember to come back when peace returns," she said and went to rush out, not to be seen by the neighbours that she was talking with a suspected Capricorn.

"Mrs. Gondwe?" said Godwin.

The woman turned back.

"I have things here, things for my wife. Can you take them? Can you hold them for me?"

He showed her the cutlery, the new bedding, the pots and the kitchen utensils. Mrs Gondwe faltered. "You can use them," said Godwin. "But if we return we can take them back then, yes?"

Mrs Gondwe nodded and began to pick up the items. She said she would return later to fetch the rest of the things. It pained him to see the brand new items, untouched by his wife, being carried off by his neighbour, but if he left it, if the house was ransacked, there would be nothing left.

Better Mrs Gondwe's hands than the hands of rioters.

Godwin was tempted to flee by bicycle but realised it would attract attention. Who didn't know Mwalimu's bicycle in Matero? He left by a footpath behind his house. Up ahead, he saw a rowdy crowd in the distance where public meetings were held. The crowd were fighting and lashing out at several policemen. The officers hit back at the unruly mob with short batons. The crowd threw stones, shouting. So that's where the police and ambulance had been heading. "*Ipayeni Ba makobo*. Kill the traitors!" The voices carried on the wind. Makobo was a tasteless fish that never struggled when caught in a net. Sell-outs to the colonial British masters were nicknamed *Ba makobo*.

He crossed Stanley Road and took another path into town. He didn't know where he was going, and it was getting dark. He passed a Jewish store where a fat Jew, Mr Goldberg, sat behind the counter laughing with some Africans. Mr Goldberg was popular among Africans because he gave goods on credit. They had nicknamed him "*Bwana Veranda*" because he liked sitting on the veranda watching people pass by. Near the shop under a streetlight, a head-shaven *Korekore* guitarist was strumming at his instrument and singing in Shona.

Godwin remembered the lines. The song was about a night train that carried children marked by the sign of the cross. The guitarist was warning mothers to be wary of black men in ties who had sold themselves to vampire men for half crown. The lines ran:

Imagine just for half crown
Only half crown
And Capricorn's heart starts to beat
He turns against his mother
Against his brother
And marks your child with the sign of the cross
To be put on that night train to Salisbury
Only for a half crown
He is not our friend
He wears a tie and eats with Whites.

Godwin's stomach rumbled. He saw a solitary woman selling buns and Coca-Cola under a mango tree and headed towards the stall. He heaved the suitcase and realised that his money was in a pair of the trousers that he had hastily packed.

He placed the suitcase on the ground and started removing the contents. A book slipped out of the suitcase, exposing a card. It was a book he had got from Mr Chanda. Godwin picked up the card and read: "Capricorn African Society, CAS; the bearer is a paid member of the CAS".

He stood rooted to the ground, unable to believe what he was seeing. So Mr Chanda *was* a member of the pro-Federation Party that had recruited Africans to champion the Federation. But was he a vampire man too?

Godwin remembered their conversations, how Mr. Chanda had laughed heartily, his eyes glinting. All along, he had fooled everyone. It was him who brought such trouble to their school.

The woman was packing her foodstuffs in a basin. Godwin's hunger had gone now. Dejected, he headed towards the Marrapodi compound.

He had no choice now. He could not go back home. He would have to spend some time on the white man's farm as a labourer and go back to teaching when the heat was down. There were always vacancies for labourers. He would write to his wife from the farm tonight. He would tell her not to come. He would tell her that their life was on hold for now, yet again. He would not tell her about Mrs. Gondwe. That would be too much. He would save up and buy new items again. His wife deserved such things.

Mr English

Everyone called him Mr English. I found the name both chic and prestigious. I don't think anyone knew his real name. Even at my age, I realised that it was not his real name because I knew all Africans had African surnames.

I did not know how Mr English got his name, though I speculated it had to do with a signpost that he put outside his restaurant, The Old Castle, which simply read: "Ask the English". In Mala, a small, multi-racial, lumbering town, the unfathomable message seemed to have a deeper meaning.

Mr English was my uncle, though I called him "elder father" in the African sense. My English teacher, Mr Limbali, had reprimanded me for using the term "elder father", explaining that in English there was no such relationship. On the other hand, my mother had also reprimanded me for addressing Mr English as "uncle", a salutation she said distanced me from him.

I enjoyed spending time at The Old Castle, often helping to clean the place. The restaurant was isolated on a rooftop towering over the community where most black people lived. During the old colonial days, it had served as a recreation centre. The faint outlines of the words "Bantu Recreation Centre" were still visible. I sometimes wondered what it was like in those days, how it looked, and who came to sit and snack and talk? It was built on rocky ground that exposed some steel and old blocks from former construction work. My uncle lived in the room at the back of the restaurant, alone, but rumour had it that he had children in

South Africa where he had spent many years before coming back to Zambia.

One day, he paid us a visit, and I started whistling the hit song "*Aphiri Anabwera*". My mother pulled a face at me, and I knew it was a warning for me to stop, an admonition not to whistle in the presence of adults.

Our guest was seated in the lime-green Morris chair, his bent right leg resting on his left knee. He gesticulated like a preacher conducting a church service. I sat in a wooden chair enjoying the conversation between Mother and our strange relative. They talked about many things that had happened in the past, reminiscing with longing.

My uncle talked about the Kwacha losing value compared to the pound which had been used shortly after independence. He also complained of too many people leaving the villages to look for work in town. In the past, whites controlled the movements of Africans. "You didn't just leave your hut with your patched trousers to go to town," he said, steadying himself in his seat. Then, changing the subject, he said, "Mother of Penza," his face breaking into a smile, which it rarely did, "Remember how I used to top the class before I was stopped from going to school to help with herding cattle?"

"I do remember. Father meant well—"

"No! I will never forgive him!" Uncle blurted, uncrossing his legs and slightly stomping his right foot to the ground. "He shouldn't—"

"Remember you were father's favourite's son," Mother said, cutting Uncle off.

"Hmm."

"We all envied the love Father showered on you."

"Nonsense. May his soul burn in hell."

"Oh now… don't say that."

Uncle did not answer. He shook his head sadly, and his face turned into a grotesque mask as if he had remembered something bad. He sighed and looked up at a faded black-and-white photograph of Mum with some people I didn't know. I had never asked her about it. He stood and got the picture frame, which was held by a piece of string. A spider that had been hiding behind it ran up the roof. Uncle looked at the picture, his face changing expressions. He put back the picture frame and bade farewell by bowing slightly in Mother's direction and raising his arm in mine.

When our guest had gone, mother lambasted me for whistling the offensive song. I understood why. The song was about a man who had left home and stayed abroad for many years until he grew very old. When he went back home with an empty suitcase, he found most of his relatives had died. I realised there was great similarity between the man in the song and my uncle.

One Saturday, I went to Mr English's restaurant to while away time. The place was kept spotlessly clean. I liked how the walls were painted a shade of blue that matched the plastic utensils and napkins on the tables. A few pictures hung on the wall. One was of the coronation of the Queen of England. The other was a full picture of Mr English in an executive black suit, complete with a white handkerchief peeping jauntily from his breast pocket. His large pants made him look like Charlie Chaplin in *The Tramp*. He stared out of the picture, his big ears protruding comically from his head. He had deep-set eyes that seemed to bore into you, his thick spectacles enhancing his serious look. He wore a pensive expression, like someone who was bored with the business of existence. As I stared at the picture, I realised how much he had changed. In the picture, he had hope.

Once, I had overheard my mother telling her friend, Mrs Siame, that Mr English had worked as a cook for several white families in South Africa. She said his homecoming to Zambia without his children depressed him, though he seemed to be more disenchanted with life at home compared to South Africa. He condemned everything under the black government. With him, it was always, "Nothing can work under a black government" or "Why did UNIP chase whites at independence; you couldn't have had all these problems if we had whites," and "There is nothing good that a black man can do."

When he was not at work in his restaurant or at home, listening to the radio, Mr English would don a battered trilby hat and take a stroll through the small wood, tapping his cane rhythmically on the ground. He would occasionally pause and look at a flower or a butterfly, bending over it as if deep in thought.

His radio, a sky-blue Grundig radio that was clearer than any radio I had heard, was ordinarily tuned to some foreign station, usually the BBC. He especially liked their programme *Focus on Africa*. I knew to keep quiet whenever he was listening to it.

Since coming back to Mala, Mr English had quickly established a reputation as being anti-UNIP, the ruling political party, and a frank critic of what he termed the "African problem". Whenever there was negative news on any African country on BBC, Mr English would point at his arm and shake his head sadly muttering, "*Ii nkanda te sana*" – This skin is not good enough.

Many people in the area secretly considered him brave, though not everybody was impressed with his frankness. Sometimes he made comments that could put him in danger with the authorities. The ruling party called all critics of the government "dissidents" or "enemies of the people". It was the period when nationalists in neighbouring countries like Southern Rhodesia and Mozambique were fighting for self-governance with the backing of the Zambian government. The party had an official security wing of thugs called vigilantes who were known for taking people "by air", literally lifting them off the ground for a beating. I would see them dressed in *chitenge* tunics, bearing the head of Kaunda or a flaming fire at UNIP rallies, marching in our community, shouting patriotic slogans. Mr English called these thugs "rascals", one of his favourite English words. The other word he was fond of was "ridiculous", which he pronounced as "roodclous".

Many people in the area considered Mr. English very educated. He regularly purchased copies of the *English Daily* and the *Times of Zambia* to keep pace with what was happening in the country. Later, as I furthered my education, passing on to secondary school, I started questioning his English, which at one time I had thought was flawless.

He was reading the *Times of Zambia,* which had a banner headline "Obote Ousted". He read quietly but audibly, "Obote… Obote." I realised that he could not read the word "ousted", but he somehow knew that Obote, the former Ugandan president, had been overthrown in a military coup. He kept muttering, "Oh too bad for the poor fellow."

Suddenly, he seemed aware of my presence and thrust the paper at me. "Heh, read for yourself what is happening to

141

the African continent since black rascals started ruling themselves." I missed the paper and it dropped onto the floor. He picked it up quickly and shouted, "Look, what you are doing! You are making my paper dirty!" He handed it over to me after dusting it carefully. "Now read," he commanded. "When I tell you blacks cannot rule themselves, you say I am out of my mind."

I read aloud, beginning with the headline, realising that in asking me to do so, Mr English was looking for a greater understanding of the information. I paused as I went along to explain the meaning of various more complicated paragraphs even though he pretended not to listen. Once I finished, he reprimanded me for speaking too loudly. "Read like the English, boy, gently and with decorum. Remember, you are not shouting about at the market. What kind of education are you young people getting nowadays?"

Despite his criticism, I could see that he was satisfied with my delivery and interpretation of the story.

I turned from looking at the pictures to see him emerging from the back office. "A cup of tea?" he asked in English, his lanky frame disappearing behind the counter.

"Yes," I answered in English, then I quickly added, "Please," before he could reprimand me for forgetting my manners.

"Sugar?" His tone was mischievous as if he knew my near gaffe.

I hesitated at his offer, fearing another, different reprimand if I said I took my tea with sugar. However, I could not bear the bitterness of tea without it, and after some hesitation, I said "Yes please, two sugars," emphasising the word "please".

He let out a baritone laughter, bending double and clutching his stomach. I was confused at his outburst until I realised the cause for his humour. Despite saying two sugars I had flashed five fingers, meaning I took five spoons of sugar in my tea. When he later came back with a steaming cup of tea, he was still laughing. The tea was sweetened to my liking.

He was in a good mood. He never usually offered me anything to drink and only asked me to help with urgent chores in the restaurant.

As I sipped my tea, he busied himself with cleaning, mopping the floor and dusting the tables. The girl who served and cooked walked in and put on an apron that was hung behind the counter.

Patrons started coming into the restaurant. A well-dressed couple pushing a baby in a pram sat in the corner and scanned the menu written on a blackboard on the wall. *Chicken and chips, K1,50; Chicken and rice, K1,50; Hamburger with tea, 50 Ngwee; Pies, 50 Ngwee with tea or coffee.* The wall was full of small hand printed messages. One read, "We are taking long in order to save you better". I always had an urge to remind Mr English about the misspelling of "save" instead of "serve", but I feared it would lead to a quarrel. Another message read, "Mr Cash was murdered by Mr Credit", accompanied by a picture drawing of Mr Credit with boxing gloves standing over a bleeding Mr Cash sprawled on the mat. There was also a picture of mountain scenery by some amateur artist. The mountains were painted green and the sky blue; no nonsense about shading.

A few months ago, during school holidays, I went to his restaurant and found it closed. This was strange, since it was a Saturday and it would ordinarily have been packed. A notice that appeared to have been hastily stuck on the door read: "Restrant closed. To open on Monday. Sorry for the trouble". I went back home and told my mother, who explained that Mr English's licence had been revoked because the place operated illegally.

A month later, the restaurant reopened, and I found Mr English in his office, which was marked, "Private". He was doing some figures in a big ledger book. Without looking up, he greeted me and asked how my mother was. I told him she was in good health. He put the book away and, getting up, began to pace about the restaurant. He was sweating. The restaurant was hot.

As usual, he was nattily dressed in an executive suit. He always wore a suit, regardless of the weather, arguing that a gentleman had no weather, another of his favourite dicta. I could smell beans cooking from the kitchen and a fainter odour of insect killer. If Mr English ever saw one fly, he got the poison from the counter and angrily sprayed at it until it dropped, and then he would sweep the poor insect away.

"I went to court," he suddenly burst out. "The case came wash out, yes wash out! They close my restaurant because I don't have a UNIP card. Why? Roodclous!" he shouted, smiling at the turn of events.

I later learnt some UNIP party member had reported Mr English's anti-party rhetoric and influenced some authorities to close his restaurant. Mr English had hired a lawyer and won the case. He talked about the victory to customers and anyone who cared to listen. I asked my mother what "wash out" meant. She explained that Mr English had been acquitted.

After our tea, I got to cleaning and wiping down tables. The baby in the pram began to cry and the woman lifted the child out and put it on her knee as she ate her chips. A man came in and sat on his own, poring over the menu carefully.

Outside, a Zambia Information Services (ZIS) Land Rover with a giant megaphone mounted on top came into view. The van moved slowly past the windows like a hearse. It had posters of Kaunda and the local parliamentary candidate pasted on it. The announcer was asking people to vote wisely. "Vote for a man of peace. Zambia is a lucky country which has never known violence. If you vote for the enemy, the party will find out and make your life miserable."

Mr. English had mocked these elections as unfair since President Kaunda stood against a symbol. "You people are mad," he said now in a voice full of contempt. He turned from the window as the van disappeared around the corner. "How can you allow a man to stand with a frog? It is roodclous. Totally roodclous."

I don't know if he was addressing the couple with the baby or the lone diner who kept looking at the menu without raising his head, but when he realised that his addressees were not keen in joining the discussion, Mr English continued muttering to himself: "All these years he has been in power. What has he done? Nothing! Completely nothing!"

The lone diner looked up at me and twirled his right index finger near his ear while shaking his head. I didn't know if by making the sign he meant Mr English was mad or big-headed.

Mr English, who was a member of the United Church of Zambia, attended English services at St Margaret's Church every Sunday. The English service started earlier in the morning before the vernacular one in *ciBemba*. He prided himself for attending the services in the "language of our friends", as he referred to whites.

I attended one such service with him. He sang English hymns more loudly than the other members of the congregation. His favourite hymn was "Rock of Ages", which he sang with gusto, his adam's apple warbling in his long neck. At the end of the service, he mingled, greeting people warmly in English like a politician at a rally. "Good preaching. So touching. I felt lifted in the spirit. Beautiful preaching." Then he would dramatically look at his Omega watch by pulling up his left shirt sleeve and announcing, "I have to rush home for some business."

Despite considering him anti-social, many people found him amusing and his behaviour became part of the local gossip in Mala. Anybody who was showy or pretended to be superior was accused of behaving like Mr English. A group of vigilantes from a neighbouring ward, who had been wreaking havoc in the area, policing households to gauge people's patriotism, had got wind of Mr English's anti-party stance. At election time, there was a carnival-like atmosphere of campaigning. It got Mr. English all agitated. He lost his temper quicker now than I'd ever seen him do before.

I changed the bags in the bins and brought them round the side of the restaurant. It was cold and the wind was blowing plastic bags, newspapers and other bits of rubbish into the air. I could hear the loosened corners of the poster printed with the directive "Ask the English", flapping at the front of the restaurant. The mangy dog that hung around the restaurant howled as if in protest. It barked madly at me as I approached, fixing me with a wild look.

Hearing the dog bark, my uncle put his head out the door. "Chase that damn thing from there," he shouted. "We will lose customers if we continue allowing a wretched thing like that to hang around."

I pretended to bend down as if picking up a stone, but to my surprise, the trick that had always worked before in sending the dog running did not work this time. Instead, the animal charged at me. I ran into the restaurant, panting and afraid. My Uncle stood in the doorway and stared down the dog. It barked, then, between its legs ran away.

I cleared the table for the couple with the baby and heard a shout coming from outside. "Remove that poster from the wall, please." It was my uncle.

"Why?" a husky male voice asked in a tone of authority and power.

Sensing a confrontation, I went outside. It was Bruno, the UNIP from the cadre. The poster in question displayed a photo of the UNIP parliamentary candidate, Mr Friday Mulenga, who was a popular party official who had defended his Mala constituency for several years. Beneath the image of the smiling candidate, a slogan read: "Vote for Friday Mulenga, the only man with integrity and openness". The symbol for the candidate was a hoe, a common image among UNIP candidates. There had been a campaign calling people to "Go Back to the Land and Cultivate".

Bruno, who was large and black, wore a Chitenge tunic top that also bore the candidate's message. He was Mr Mulenga's right hand man and the leader of the dreaded vigilante gang. The other candidate, Mr Samson Nkonde, wasn't very popular. I had seen a few of his posters at the market. His symbol was a hen with chicks, which meant he would care for the people the way a mother hen cared for her brood. Bruno's vigilante set was the most dreaded and notorious for using intimidating methods against "enemies of the people".

Later, I learned that Bruno had been chosen to put up posters at the restaurant because the other Party members feared my uncle.

In defiance, Bruno nailed another poster on the far corner of the restaurant. His face glistened with sweat. He had huge muscles and stood large and looming. He worked deliberately, provocatively. My uncle warned him to stop, and after repeating himself four times, rushed forward and tore the offending posters down.

Bruno confronted my uncle, pointing an accusing finger in his face. "I have heard a lot about you. You are always out to frustrate the Party's effort. This is not South Africa where whites are in control. This is Zambia, an independent state with a black leader."

"So what?"

"So what? The Party—"

"This is private property. You have no right to stick posters here," my uncle shouted in English, adding loudly, "By law, by law." He emphasised the latter statement, stomping his foot.

"*By law by law*. I have a right to put posters on this wall." He was visibly enjoying himself.

A crowd had gathered by now to witness the scene, which was entertainment in a dull place like Mala. Bruno, who seemed to know the power he wielded against my uncle, was not in a hurry to pounce on the proud "black Englishman". He light-heartedly took two posters from a bunch he was holding in his left hand and authoritatively handed them to my uncle. "Stick these in place of the ones you have removed." When my uncle hesitated, Bruno added, "Come on, Mr Gentleman, help with party work. Don't just sit in your restaurant like a big *Bwana* condemning us."

Some people in the crowd laughed. My uncle did not. He turned to the crowd and spoke in English. "Leave my premises. This is private property."

I went into the restaurant, hoping the crowd would disperse. The lone diner was staring and the couple with the baby had turned in their seats to look. From outside came a *whack, whack, whack.*

I ran back outside to see Bruno, hands working like pistons, slapping my uncle in the face. My uncle blinked and looked dazed.

"Don't hit my uncle," I shouted in English.

"Mr English has influenced the boy to speak in English," someone commented from the crowd.

The comment was met by laughter. I glanced at them and saw a mixture of fear and embarrassment for what Bruno was doing to my uncle.

Now several more vigilantes appeared from nowhere and started hitting my uncle. They rained blows on him and lifted him "by air". They bundled him into a Party van and drove away, all while my uncle shouted, "This is what I keep saying, a black man cannot rule himself. Whites don't do this." The vigilantes ignored him as the van sped off.

Filled with fear, I went back into the restaurant and saw to the customers who jumped up to leave. As I took their money and cleaned over the tables, my fear turned to anger.

Why had they done that to my uncle? I closed the restaurant and went home to tell my mother.

After spending two days in police cells, Mr. English was released without charge. I accompanied my mother to see him released. He looked haggard and twice his age. All the light was gone out of his eyes. I could see there was no hope left now at all.

A policeman called out his name, "Rueben Siame". And there it was. Mr. English's real name. We didn't talk on our way home, but I felt I knew what he was thinking.

He later closed his restaurant and left after saying a hasty goodbye one evening. I asked my mother where he had gone.

"He went back to South Africa. One of his sons called him back after he heard that he had been detained."

I missed my Uncle and his eccentric ways. I missed calling into the restaurant to help out. A few weeks after Mr. English left, the restaurant was turned into a UNIP office and a large poster of Mr. Friday Mulenga was pasted to the wall. The "Ask the English" poster was torn down. I stood and stared at Mr. Mulenga's grinning face, feeling a deep sadness for my uncle. Now there was nothing left. Now there was no trace of Mr. English at all.

Acknowledgements & Notes on the text

'Harlem', by Langstone Hughes, first published in *Montage of a Dream*, 1951
then *The Collected Works of Langston Hughes, 2002*, reprinted by permission of Harold Ober Associates Inc. Quoted in 'A Dream Deferred', from www.poetryfoundation.org in 2023.

A few stories in this collection were inspired by real characters and events. They include 'Aunt Agatha's Quest', 'The Hate That Hate Produced', 'Anna's Song', 'Mrs Skerman', and 'Maria's Vision'.

The following stories have previously been published as follows:

'Kippie Goes Home' - Published in From A to Z Diverse Voices from Zambia, Cheza Hope Foundation, Lusaka, 2017.

'Mensah's London Blues' - The New Black Magazine, 18 December 2010

'Aunt Agatha's Quest' - Munyori Literary Journal ISSN: 2168-6440

'Maria's Vision' - Africa Writing Online ISSN 1754-6672 No 5. 'Maria's Vision was also adapted to film by Zollywood Zimbabwe, in 2014.

'A Dream Deferred' - Maple Tree Literary Supplement ISSN 1916-341X

'Anna's Song' - The New Black Magazine, 13 June 2010

'The Hate That Hate Produced' - New Coin Africa Writer Magazine, 17 April 2004

'Dambudzo Marechera Writes to Samantha' was a story born from an aborted project to celebrate Dambudzo's posthumous 59th birthday in 2011. The goal was to compile an eBook anthology entitled "Remembering Marechera," consisting of essays, reviews, short stories and poems to be published by Storyline Publishing. The project was a brainchild of a white Zimbabwean writer, Ivor Hartmann, who invited submissions until the 6th of April 2011. At that time, Austin Kaluba was living in Oxford and frequented some places Dambudzo used to hang out. He did extensive research on Marechera and penned the epistolary piece included in this collection. When the project was aborted by Hartmann, Kaluba posted the story online, and it went wildly viral among Zimbabweans home and abroad, who thought the letter had been written by Marechera himself.

About the author

Austin Kaluba was born in Northern Zambia and was an editor for the *Sunday Times* of Zambia before being appointed as a diplomat to the United Kingdom, where he worked at the Zambia High Commission in London and studied Creative Writing at the University of Oxford Department for continuing education.

Drawing on the author's international experience, this collection of short stories represents a rich and varied vision of the tension between African experience in a largely "post-colonial" world, both within Africa and the diaspora. In a mood reminiscent of Alex La Guma's *A Walk in the Night*, Samuel Selvon's *The Lonely Londoners* or V.S Naipaul's *Miguel Street* the collection pulls the reader into the lives of its characters as though they were taken by the hand on a walk down a street that is in equal measures familiar and strange. With a rich variety of narrators and situations, *Mensah's London Blues and Other Stories* has many twists and moments of surprise.

Ingram Content Group UK Ltd.
Milton Keynes UK
UKHW041102140723
425131UK00004B/36

9 781914 287046